FORTIFIED

NERI MORRIS

NM//

NERI MORRIS.

FORTIFIED

This book is dedicated to all the women whose life has not turned out how they hoped and still managed to do something great for the glory of God.

Contents

Prologue   1
Preface   2
1. The Golden Goddess   3
2. The Bird   17
3. The Zwinger   29
4. The Following Night   41
5. The Little Black Book   55
6. The Piece of Paper   63
7. The Hiding Place   75
8. The Closet   89
9. The Garbage Run   95
10. The Hair Dye   107
11. The Cigar   115
12. The Sound of Sirens   127
13. The Chaos   137
14. The Need for Coffee   145
15. The Return   155

Glossary   173
About the Author   175
Also by Neri Morris   176

"So they went and entered
the house of a prostitute
named Rahab…"

Joshua 2:1

Preface

In 1945, the German war effort was on its knees. Led by Winston Churchill (code name Frankland), the Allied forces wanted to attack German morale in an attempt to bring an end to the war. Operation Thunderclap was devised as a way to deliver on this outcome. Originally, Berlin was the target of choice for the bombing but the plan was changed to focus on East German cities, including Dresden, a city that held no strategic significance.

Frankland tasked Secretary for Air, Sir Archibald Sinclair to carry out the bombing. Sinclair did not disappoint, urging Deputy Chief of the Air Staff, Sir Norman Bottomley to get "Bomber" Harris to deliver the destruction on the city of Dresden.

Two days and four air raids later, not much remained of the city of Dresden. It has taken almost 75 years for this German town to rebuild.

ONE

The Golden Goddess

25th January 1945, 9:30pm

From: Frankland.
To: Secretary of State for Air, Sir Sinclair.
Subject: Operation Thunderclap.
Coordinate a RAF air raid attack on Chemnitz, Leipzig and Dresden. To be carried out at the earliest to assist with Soviet offence. Code name "Operation Thunderclap." Also consider Berlin and other large cities.

26th January 1945, 1:03 pm

From: Secretary of State for Air, Sir Sinclair.
To: Chief of the Air Staff, Sir Portal.
Subject: New Mission - Operation Thunderclap.
Frankland has requested coordinated attack to assist Soviet offensive. Locations suggested are Chemnitz, Leipzig and Dresden. Targeting rail,

communication and any other significant targets,
How quickly can you coordinate attack?

26th January 1945, 3:54 pm

From: Chief of the Air Staff, Sir Portal.
To: Secretary of State for Air, Sir Sinclair.
Subject: Re - New Mission - Operation Thunderclap.
We should use available effort in one big attack
on Berlin and attacks on Dresden, Leipzig and
Chemnitz or any other cities where a severe
blitz will not only cause confusion in the evacuation from the East, but will also hamper the
movement of troops from the West. But no
aircraft should be diverted to carry such raids.
They should remain on current primary task of
targeting oil production facilities, factories
and submarine yards.

26th January 1945, 4:11 pm

To: Frankland
From: Secretary of State for Air, Sir Sinclair.
Subject: Re - Operation Thunderclap.
Response from Portal: We should use available
effort in one big attack on Berlin and attacks
on Dresden, Leipzig and Chemnitz or any other
cities where a severe blitz will not only cause
confusion in the evacuation from the East, but
will also hamper the movement of troops from the
West. But no aircraft should be diverted to
carry such raids. They should remain on current

primary task of targeting oil production facilities, factories and submarine yards.

26th January 1945, 4:51 pm

To: Secretary of State for Air, Sir Sinclair.
From: Frankland.
Subject: Re - Re - Operation Thunderclap.
Unsatisfactory. I asked whether Berlin, and no doubt other large cities in east Germany, should not now be considered especially attractive targets. Pray report to me tomorrow what is going to be done. Time is of the essence if we are to break German spirit and end the war.

26th January 1945, 5:49 pm

To: Deputy Chief of the Air Staff, Air Marhsall Sir Bottomley.
From: Secretary of State for Air, Sir Sinclair.
Subject: URGENT - Operation Thunderclap.
Frankland wants RAF Air raid attacks to happen A.S.A.P. Forge ahead in coordinating the attack. Get Bomber Harris onboard. Undertake attacks of Berlin, Dresden, Leipzig and Chemnitz as soon as moonlight and weather permits with the particular object of exploiting the confused conditions which are likely to exist in the above mentioned cities.

26th January 1945, 8:23 pm

To: Secretary of State for Air, Sir Sinclair.

From: Deputy Chief of the Air Staff, Air Marhsall Sir Bottomley.
Subject: Re - URGENT - Operation Thunderclap.
Bomber Harris is a go. Will report shortly on dates. Let Frankland know he will have his raids.

27th January 1945, 9:08 pm

To: Frankland.
From: Secretary of State for Air, Sir Sinclair.
Subject: Operation Thunderclap Is A Go.
Bomber is a go, Prime Minister. Confirm dates shortly. Received intel of potential secret munitions factory in Dresden. Have deployed our best spies to locate munitions factory in order to concentrate bombing in this area. Will confirm date of Raid when location confirmed.

J anuary 31st 1945, 11:34am

Ava drained her coffee, smoothing the crimson silk sheets that swirled around her legs, watching the sunlight dance across them. The sun was almost at its highest which meant she would need to get out from under these divine sheets if she was to make it in time. But for now, she slid back down, lengthening her body and spreading the full width of the bed. A few more minutes wouldn't hurt. After all, this was one of the many perks of living on her own, having the entire bed to herself. She smiled at the thought, feeling the sun warm her body. It was an unusually warm day for winter, the snow still fresh from the day before. This was Ava's favourite kind of day, cool enough to need to dress warmly but warm enough to be heated by the sun.

Her thoughts drifted to the night before. Lord Mayor Neiland had been very forthcoming in the Führer's plans, much to Ava's delight. The information he had shared with her after she had taken care of him would prove advantageous. Ava reached for the money on the nightstand, doing a quick count and folding it up. She would give it to Ayala for emergencies.

Finally surrendering to the time, Ava slid out from under her sheets, and began her hunt downstairs to get more coffee. Margot was in the kitchen, a pot already steaming on the table.

"Mmmm. That smells good." Ava smiled at her friend.

"Freshly made. I'm assuming you want some?" Margot asked, instinctively reaching for a cup.

"Yes, please." Ava eased herself into the chair, eager to delay, if only for a few minutes, having to brave the war-torn world that waited for her beyond the threshold. "Are the others up yet?" She asked through a yawn.

"Olga is already out, not entirely sure where she ran off to this morning. Zara and Heidi are still asleep, and I heard Tilly's wireless going, so I assume that means she is awake." Margot placed the coffee in front of Ava. It was one of the small indulgences she allowed the girls, paying whatever she had to in order to make sure they had one of the few luxuries their lifestyle afforded them.

"Last night was a good night." Margot commented, taking the seat across from Ava, brushing a strand of those gorgeous red curls the boys loved so much from her face.

"It was. Especially considering how cold it was outside. I almost expected no man to brave the weather." Ava took a sip, savouring the moment. "But tonight may be even bigger. I heard whisperings that there is a truck load of new troops arriving today and we all know they're going to be hungry." She winked at Margot.

"I love the hungry ones," Margot smiled. "They always tip better than the regulars. Did Richter tell you that?"

Ava took another sip. "No, I overheard Müller, one of Killinger's men, mention it."

"Ahh, it would seem Richter's little kolibri is doing her job." Margot teased.

Ava shot her a fiery look. "Don't call me that." Margot raised her hands, knowing she had hit a nerve. "Sorry." She quickly replied. "Bad joke." Margot paused. "I still don't get why he calls you a Hummingbird. I would think a Starling would be more appropriate, don't you?"

Ava sighed, the good mood she was in quickly fading. The last thing she wanted to do was to talk about Richter. "I don't know why he calls me 'kolibri' and I don't care to know." She drained the last of her coffee. "I need to go."

She stood, signalling the end of the conversation and made her way upstairs. The sound of Tilly's wireless caught her thoughts as she made her way down the hall. The sweet, crackling music reminded her of simpler times, a longing growing inside her for the small house at the edge of the city that had been her home and her haven. If only Papa had not died, then maybe life would have turned out differently. The pain of old wounds being pressed on swelled with Ava's stomach and she pushed the memories from her mind again. Mama would be expecting her shortly and she needed to hurry. Ava carefully pieced herself together, each decision from what dress she wore to how she set her hair, measured and thought out. She would stand out in a crowd no matter what she dressed in but that didn't mean she would try to blend in either. The more she played her role, the less likely anyone would pay attention to what she was hiding. It was all smoke and mirrors.

Ava stepped out onto the snow, fixing her gloves and pulling her coat tighter around her. Taking a deep breath in, she squared her shoulders back and lifted her head high. Releasing the breath, she began her journey.

"Hallo Schönheit, you want to come upstairs?" A man jeered, a toothless smile and a wink conveying his message loud and clear. Ignoring his request, Ava continued her journey, pulling her coat tighter. Such open invitations were not uncommon for her. She was propositioned so frequently on the street that it simply rolled off her back. Ava knew she was beautiful. She had been told as such since she was a child and it was partly why she could draw the numbers she did every night. Men came from all over the city to the Zwinger Bordell to see the high-priced courtesan, the Goldene Götten. The Golden Goddess. Aptly named because of her golden locks, pristine complexion and perfect curves. Ava was the desire of every man and the envy of every woman. Wives dragged their husbands in the opposite direction when they passed her on the street. And husbands wasted no time propositioning her when their wives were out of sight. A night with the Golden Goddess cost more than most men earned in a month but was rumoured to be worth every cent.

Ava had never set out to become a courtesan but the profession served her well, providing a lifestyle most women would never be able to enjoy. A profession she wondered, as she looked up at the apartment block, if her mother would ever truly forgive her for. Ava pressed on the door to the building and climbed the three flights of stairs to the top apartment, letting herself in. It hadn't been easy finding somewhere to hide her family, but money opened doors that otherwise would have remained shut and she had purchased the tiny flat at a premium, primarily for the small attic space off the second bedroom. It was undetectable, camouflaged by the wall panelling that disguised its entrance. It hid her family well, as had been proven by the unexpected raid the Nazis had carried out a year earlier. They rounded up all the Jews left in the city and paraded them down the main street, like a lion showing off its kill, never to be seen again. The memory chilled Ava's bones. It had been a dark day for Dresden.

Thankfully, Ava's family had remained safe, hidden behind the secret walls of the attic and a carefully maintained facade Ava kept. Just another way her profession served her well. She was mysterious and secretive by reputation, so her daily visits to an apartment not far from the Zwinger were perceived as not out of character.

"It's me." She called out softly, slipping off her shoes. Bare feet only and low voices always, so as to not draw attention. So far, they had lived in the flat for almost 2 years undetected and Ava intended to keep it that way. At least until the war was over. Whenever that would be.

"Tanté Ava!" Levi, her 6 year old nephew, wrapped himself around her legs.

"Hallo Levi." She knelt down, engulfing him in a hug. "How are you today?" She asked.

"I am well. But bored. Mama is making me read." He rolled his eyes and showed her his book.

"Ah, a very good skill to have." Ava smiled. "What are you reading?"

"A book about birds." He said, flipping the book open. An image caught Ava's attention.

"Ooo, do you know what this bird is, Levi?" Ava pointed to the page. Levi shook his head. "This is a Rosenfink. It is a little finch with a bright red chest and head."

"Why would I need to know that?" Her strong-willed nephew asked. "I do not care about birds. Or reading. I like neither."

Ava smiled. "If you want to be a pilot one day, mein lamm, you will need to know how to read."

Levi paused, a furrow forming in his brow, deep in thought. "I will become a doctor then!" He declared, thrusting a pointed hand in the air as though he had solved a mystery. Ava chuckled. "Oh Levi, you will need to know how to read for that too. In fact, any job you wish to have when you are older, will require you to read."

Defeat entered his body. "Really?"

"Yes, mein lamm."

"Then I shall not have a job!" He triumphantly exclaimed. Believing he had won the argument, he turned on his heel and ran back to his toys. Ava stood, chuckling to herself, he will make a great politician one day.

"Hallo Hadar." Ayala appeared from the kitchen, embracing her sister.

"Ayala, we have talked about this." Ava whispered sternly into her sister's ear. "You need to call me Ava. That is my name. I stopped being called Hadar a long time ago."

"Ah," Ayala threw her hands in the air. "I know, I know. But you can't fault me for calling my sister by the name she was born with!"

Ava shot Ayala an unimpressed glance as she removed her gloves. "Where's Mama?" Ava asked, taking off her coat and looking past Ayala down the hall.

"She is in her room, reading. Mama! *Ava* is here." Ayala called out, winking as she emphasised Ava's name and taking her coat from her.

"Hallo Ava." Hila emerged from her room, giving Ava a hug devoid of the warmth her mother's arms once held.

"Hallo Mama." Ava returned the hug, wishing it felt more like home. "How are you today?"

"Oh I am fine, same as always." Hila walked into the kitchen. "Tea?" she asked. Ava ignored the forced politeness in her voice, eager to share with them the package in her bag. "I have something better." She replied, pulling out a small tin of coffee from her purse. Hila and Ayala's eyes grew wide.

"How did you get that?" Ayala took the tin from Ava, inhaling deeply the fragrance that spilled forth.

"I ordered a little extra this week. As a gift. Business has been going well and I wanted to bring you something more than bread and milk." Ava smiled at the joy on Ayala's face. A smile that quickly diminished when she saw her mother turn her back. Hila had never taken well to Ava's choice of profession but that didn't change her love and care for her mother. "Mama. Come now, enjoy the gift." Ava pleaded, taking the coffee back and walking over to her mother. "It is a gift. Why does it matter how I came about the means to buy it?" She asked, knowing full well the answer.

"Good Jewish girls do not do what you do." Hila tersely whispered.

"This may be true Mama, but good Jewish girls will also do what they need to do, to keep their family alive." Ava turned her mother to face her. "I know you worry, but your Yahweh has blessed me with the features of a German and a place of business where it matters little your heritage. We need to leverage that. You are too old to work, and Joseph and Levi need their mother. Plus, it's not safe for any of you to be out on the street. If they find out you are Jewish, you will be sent to a concentration camp."

"Is it any safer for you?" Hila shot back.

"No Mama, it is not. But someone has to protect you and that is what I'm doing."

"By bringing shame on our family name. By selling yourself to the highest bidder." Angry tears formed at the corners of Hila's eyes. Tears that broke Ava's heart. Would she ever understand?

"By doing what I must for the people I love." Ava sighed. "I don't expect you to understand Mama, but I do want you to know my motives. Papa is gone and Benjamin is missing. Someone has to take care of you all. During these times does it really matter how it's done?"

"You were doing this before the war. Do not use the war as your excuse." Hila spat out.

"I'm not using the war. My reasons for doing what I do are the same. Papa died, Mama, we were struggling."

"You think I could ever forget!" Hila snapped back, turning her back to Ava.

Ava let out a sigh, steadying herself, remembering that Levi was in the other room. She turned Hila towards her. "Mama, I know you don't approve and I have come to terms with that. If you can't accept what I do, at least acknowledge why I do it."

Hila looked up into Ava's eyes. She sensed the slightest softening in her mother's resolve. But just as quickly as she had glimpsed it, the softening was gone and replaced with the disapproving hardness Ava had come to expect from her mother.

"You are your own person Hadar. You make your decisions. If the Germans find out who you are then that is on you." Hila looked away. "I just hope Yahweh can forgive you." She not so subtlety mumbled under her breath. Ava went to bite back but paused instead. She wasn't sure it mattered much what Yahweh thought. He had given up on her a long time ago, so she had repaid in kind.

But that didn't change the fact that her mother and sister still believed Yahweh cared about them and out of love and respect for them, she would play along.

"And I believe that Yahweh will understand one day why I do what I do." Ava responded. "Now, shall we have some coffee?" Ava reached for the open tin and waved it under her mother's nose, teasing her with the smell. The hint of a smile formed at the corners of Hila's lips. "I will put the kettle on." She replied, leaving the conversation swept under the rug, with everything else that remained unsaid.

Ava handed her mother the coffee and sat down with Ayala. The lines of fatigue and worry etched into her sister's face tugged at Ava's heart. She glanced in her mother's direction, Hila's back was towards her daughters as she focussed on the brewing coffee. Ava reached into her pocket and took Ayala's hand, pressing the wad of cash into her sister's palm. Ayala's eyes grew wide at the sizeable amount of money. Pressing a finger to her lips, Ava signalled the exchange was to remain a secret. Ayala nodded and quickly shoved the money into pocket.

"Any word about Benjamin?" Ava asked, already knowing the answer.

"Nein. Not a single sound." Ayala glanced in the direction of her son. "It's been almost three years since he went missing. Joseph misses him deeply. Sometimes I wonder if Levi remembers him at all." Ayala sighed as she watched her youngest son play. "I see him in their eyes and my heart breaks at the thought that he may never get to see them grow up." Her voice broke slightly and Ava reached again for her hand, wishing she could do more to comfort her sister than bring coffee and give her money. Ava had hoped that news of Benjamin's whereabouts would surface through the many conversations she was privy to at the Zwinger but nothing had come her way. It's like he just disappeared without a trace.

"Tanté!" Ava turned at the sound of her eldest nephew's voice as Joseph came into the kitchen, his presence quickly shifting the topic of conversation.

"Here's my favourite nine-year-old nephew! Come give your Tanté a hug." She held out her arms.

"What about me!?" Levi protested from the lounge room. Ava chuckled as she let Joseph go. "You are my favourite six-year-old nephew." She winked and turned back. "Now, Joseph, tell me, what has your Mama been teaching you today?"

January 31st 1945, 2:51pm

Nathan Sinclair breathed hot air into his hands as he waited for his partner, Eddie Flannagen, to retrieve the letter. German winters seemed colder to the British spy, or maybe it was just the chill of this godforsaken war. Either way, he'd take a dreary London day over the German chill that seemed to have permanently set in his bones, any day.

A truck load of troops screamed around the corner, catching Nathan's attention. It screeched to a halt just off to his left, followed by two more. Troops began to pile out of all three trucks, as Nathan artfully slipped around the corner, positioning himself close enough to listen but not be seen.

"Schneider! Get me some smokes!" Nathan heard one of the troops yell. He peered around the corner to see two German Luffewaffe soldiers standing where he had been only a moment earlier. Pressing his back up against the wall, he listened.

"Are you going to go?" The smaller solider asked the other.

"Of course I'm going to go. We're in Dresden. It's the only thing to do."

"Do you think she'll be there?"

"She's always there. But she isn't going to give you the time of day, dummkopf!" One of them jeered the other.

"Why's that?"

"Because she is going to be spending the whole night with a real man!"

"Who? Lieutenant General Richter?" The smaller soldier mocked.

"Nein! Me!"

"No chance. I hear she spends all her time with the Lieutenant General."

"Truppen! In the truck! Jetzt!" The commanding officer yelled. They immediately scurried off, the trucks roaring to life and take off around the corner. Nathan surfaced from his hiding place, watching as the trucks sped off. He resumed his position against the wall, the conversation between the two troops playing in his mind. He wasn't sure why, but something about it lingered. 'Help me to see what you want me to see.' Nathan silently prayed, as he scanned the conversation again and again.

"Auf wiedersehen!" Eddie called out as he exited the bookstore, the sound of the bell catching Nathan's attention. He looked up at Eddie who gave him a slight nod. Shifting his weight off the wall, Nathan began walking down the street, Eddie quickly falling in step next to him.

"Let's get some tea." Nathan said, the two-men walking the rest of the way in silence.

TWO

The Bird

January 31st 1945, 3:12pm

Ava visited for as long as she could, but as the afternoon wore on, she knew she needed to get back to the Zwinger. If what she had heard the night before was true, then she wanted to make sure the bar, and the girls, were ready.

"Ok, mein Liebchens, Tanté has to go, come give me cuddles." Ava held out her arms to her two nephews, breathing in their innocence as she held them tight. She would do anything to keep them safe. If it was within her power, she would get them out of Germany altogether. But what hope had she of smuggling her Jewish family out of Nazi Germany? She hated keeping them locked away but the thought of losing them forever was too much. It didn't seem to matter that they were third generation German citizens. They were Jewish and that had sealed their fate. Ava's nephews squirmed out of her extra long embrace and went back to their studies. She straightened as her sister helped her put on her coat.

"Put that money somewhere safe and remember only go out if you absolutely need to and only to the places I have told you. Make sure you are covered from head to toe and not followed."

Ayala rolled her eyes. "Yes boss." She responded mockingly.

"I'm serious." Ava pressed.

"So am I." Ayala pushed back. "We know the drill. Besides, you have given us plenty of food for now, so I don't see there being any reason for us to leave the cage." She winked and smiled warmly at her older sister.

"Ok, I'll be back tomorrow." Ava looked down the hall. "I'm going Mama!" she called out in a low voice.

Hila came out of the kitchen, wiping her hands on her apron. "Auf wiedersehen." She hugged Ava. "Please, my girl, be careful." She whispered into her ear.

"I will Mama, I promise." She kissed her mother on the cheek and slipped out the door.

Ava stepped out onto the street and pulled on her gloves, a fluttering sound to her left catching her attention. She smiled in surprise as a little Rose Finch landed on the windowsill of the ground floor apartment. She stood there for a moment, watching the little finch hop around on the sill. 'How coincidental to see the little bird for a second time that day?' Ava thought to herself. Thinking nothing more of it, she began the walk through the dreary, war-burdened streets of Dresden. This city, that once had been bursting with life, was more like a white-washed tomb. A shining jewel on the outside, but on the inside, in the streets, it was dead. Food was scarce. Kindness forgotten. Death at the forefront of everyone's mind. Ava's heart ached for what once was.

The bird on the windowsill appeared in her mind, itself a reminder of a simpler, quieter time, when life was slower and her family complete. As a little girl she would play for hours in the woods across the meadow from their small family home, chasing the little finches, mesmerised by their quick movements and bold colour. She had desperately wanted one as a pet, remembering how her Papa had chuckled when she had asked for one. Ava spent a whole week listing over and over again all the reasons a Rosenfink would make a very useful pet. But money was tight and with no way of catching one, let alone caring for the bird long term, Ava's hopes remained unfulfilled. Instead, her Papa had come home one afternoon with a little cardboard box. He proudly handed it to her saying that for now, this little trinket would have to do. She opened the box to find a small Rosenfink pin. Papa had knelt down beside her, taking the pin from the box and attaching it to her dress, saying "Now, mein lamm, every time you look at this pin, remember how much your Papa loves you, how brave you are, just like this finch. Do not be fooled by his size, for he is fast and smart and strong. Just like you." He kissed the tip of her nose and stood up. Ava didn't take the brooch off for a year.

She smiled at the memory, resolving that tonight she would wear her little Rosenfink pin and focus on the joy of that moment she had shared with her Papa, ignoring the guilt it summoned within her. Ava rounded the corner and looked up the hill, the Zwinger now in sight. She let out a sigh as her mother's words annoyingly floated back into her mind. She knew opening a brothel was not what Yahweh would have wanted. She knew it was dangerous work. She knew the stakes were high, given her heritage . She knew that her family worried for her safety and were equally ashamed of her profession. But if there was one thing Ava was good at, it was making men feel like men. Strong. Needed. Lusted after. Desired. A skill she had learned out of necessity.

Her family had been torn apart by the sudden death of her father, the tragedy sending them into greater financial hardship. Her mother, who had never worked outside of the home, had to quickly find employment and the little she made barely covered the basics. It wasn't long before the 'For Sale' sign went up on their small family home and they moved into a small flat in the city. Soon after moving into the city, Ava met Sabine, a girl who was a little older then her and spent a lot of time on their street corner. Sabine had been the first to introduce Ava to a world where her looks could be used to make money. Fuelled by anger at Yahweh and filled with guilt over the death of her father, Ava sought recompense by taking responsibility for the wellbeing of her family and Sabine provided a way to do that.

Initially she had told her mother she was working in a dress shop. But it hadn't taken long for the whispers in the streets to make their way to her mother and Hila soon figured out that where there is smoke, there is fire. She had been furious with Ava, the shame of it all had sent her into a rage, yelling and crying, demanding Ava stop. But Ava refused, believing this was how she was meant to pay for what had happened to Papa. Hila had thrown her out.

Ava had stayed with Sabine for a short while, learning all the ways to pleasure a man without ending up pregnant or with a disease, even how she too, could enjoy the work. As the months wore on, the person Ava once was became a distant memory. Hadar faded into the background and Ava emerged from the ashes, seeking to put to death who she used to be and what she had done, in favour of creating a new identity.

But a change in name could not remove the division between her and her mother, which stretched on for years. Ava continued to send money to Ayala, despite her mother's rejection. It had taken the birth of Joseph to direct the family towards the path of restoration and healing. A journey they were still on.

Ava had always been stringently careful, soon realizing her looks attracted a clientele that was willing to shower her with gifts and luxuries the lower class men could never afford. She went from labourers and farmers to Politicians, high-powered businessmen and film moguls, quickly earning her the nickname the Goldene Götten. An image that was cemented when she purchased the Zwinger. An image she used to her advantage every night. An image that shielded her true identity.

Ava pushed her weight against the kitchen door. Removing her coat and gloves, she made her way into the saloon, going about her nightly routine. While living the courtesan life had its perks, someone still needed to set up for the evenings trade and keep an eye on things. Ava liked being the Madame, only granting access to her bed when a true high-paying client walked through the door. She had learned quite early on in her career that stroking a man's ego, plying him with liquor and providing him something to chase had the same effect as stroking another part of a man's body. Both made a man feel alive. Both made them feel like they were *the* man. Both left a man wanting more. The only difference was one required less effort than the other. Plus, alcohol had a bigger profit margin.

So, Ava spent her evenings swooning over the men that came through the door, flirting with them, whispering sweet nothings in their ear, while leaving the heavy lifting to her girls. Her very well-paid girls. Ava made sure they were well compensated for their work, providing not just a room, food and a wage but a family and a home. Ava had been adamant about that when she bought the place. It wasn't just a palace of pleasure, it was a safe place for women who had seen no other option. Ava knew well the state of desperation and need these women were in to make the decisions they had, and she cast no judgement. Understanding and safety were what they needed and Ava provided both. She knew deep down if there had been another way, all of them would have chosen a different path. But there hadn't been. Their only choice now was conducting business in a safe, comfortable bed or an alleyway.

She picked up a damp cloth and began to wipe down the bar, checking the bottles of liquor and making a mental note of what she needed to re-stock. A palace of pleasure needed an endless fountain of liquor to keep everyone playing nice. Ava paused, letting her eyes scan the saloon. She had chosen the name "Zwinger Bordell" because of the dual purpose of a Zwinger. In times of peace, a Zwinger was used as a garden, providing a place of serenity and pleasure. In times of war, it was a kill zone, an offensive tactic to overrun the enemy from above.

Was her establishment a place for pain or for pleasure in the middle of this never-ending war? She couldn't tell. Maybe it was both. If Ava had learned anything over her years in this business, there was no pleasure without pain. The Zwinger had become a place of enjoyment amidst the pain. A place to forget, even for an hour, that the world was burning outside.

Ava heard the front door open and glanced at the clock. Right on time.

"Hallo Otto!" She called out, reaching for a glass and pouring him a beer.

"Guten tag Ava, how are you today?" Otto ambled into the saloon as he did every day at 5:30pm and eased himself onto the stool at the end of the bar. Same time, same spot, every day.

"I am well. You are looking especially fine this evening. Is that a new shirt?" Ava asked, handing him the beer with a wink.

"Oh Ava, you know it's not. No one can afford anything with this bloody war. But thank you for saying that. Proost!" He nodded, tipping his glass towards Ava and taking a sip. "The best in town as always."

"I'll leave you to enjoy it in peace." She smiled and made her way upstairs. She liked Otto, he was kind and sweet. Never wanted anything other than to come in for a quiet beer before he began his round as their local garbage collector. He was always on time, paid before he left and never disturbed the girls.

"Ava!" She turned at the sound of her name to see Olga poking her head out of her bedroom door. "Is that Otto?" She whispered, the joy in her voice noticeable despite her attempt to conceal it. Ava nodded and continued walking, a smile forming on her lips. Olga thought Ava didn't see the affection she had for the garbage man, but there was little under this roof, if anything, that went unnoticed by Ava. So long as their connection didn't interfere with trade, Ava had no issue with it.

She let herself into the bathroom, locking the door behind her as the need to escape for a while swelled within her. Ava turned on the water and watched the steam roll into the air around her. She poured rose scented soap into the bath and waited as the steam lifted the fragrance to her nostrils. Ava took a long, deep breath and let the sweet aroma take her away to a field of flowers in her mind where she lingered, forgetting reality for a single moment.

Ava undressed and eased herself into the water, enjoying the sensation of weightlessness and stillness, the meadow of flowers a distant, blurry image as her thoughts drifted to the evening ahead. She was going to need all the strength she could muster tonight. While her lifestyle allowed her to live as she pleased and surround herself with luxuries, it also meant she was privy to many of the secret dealings of the rich and influential. Information was the most powerful commodity and that had never been more true then now. Information was everything in this war.

Ava lowered her head under the water, losing herself in the silence, relishing the precious few moments of peace before the nights trade began. The Lieutenant General was coming tonight, and he was going to want what Ava knew.

January 31st 1945, 3:24pm

"What's it say?" Eddie asked, pouring the hot water into the tea pot.

"They want the location of the secret munitions factory by week's end." Nathan replied, closing the cipher and putting the encrypted letter back inside the jacket cover of the book. He slid the book onto the shelf with the rest of the collection, hiding the cipher under the floorboards of their dreary apartment, south of the Elbe river.

"By week's end?" Eddie's eyes grew wide with frustration. "Do they think this information is just written on some sign somewhere? Caw blimey!" He took a frustrated sip and shook his head. "It could take weeks before we're embedded enough to find the location!"

"Calm down, Eddie." Nathan stared out the dingy apartment window that overlooked the miserable street below, watching a small, red bird hop around in the snow. Eddie was right, they had been in Dresden for a little over two days, nowhere near long enough to embed themselves properly and flush out the information. The urgency was surprising. And a little unsettling.

"Should we scout out those factories we came across yesterday?" Eddie's question drew Nathan's attention.

"Yeah, maybe." Nathan eased himself into the chair across from Eddie, pondering the assignment they had been given.

"You don't seem very confident in that being our first step, old chap." Eddie observed.

"Because I'm not." He sipped his tea. "It just makes no strategic sense to put an underground munitions factory in that location. It's the furthest point away from the railway and too close to the main comms building." The two men sat in silence. Nathan's mind began to run through what they knew so far of the roads and streets of Dresden, mentally searching for any clue or sign that this city held an underground munitions factory designed to fuel the German war effort in the north east. They were yet to find a single piece of useful information as to the whereabouts of the factory and if it actually existed. The search was proving more difficult than they anticipated and this deadline only added to the pressure.

On previous missions, they had be in and out within twenty-four to thirty-six hours, intel obtained and on it's way to the Allied forces as they disappeared into the gun smoke, their next assignment in hand. They were shadows, masters at extracting information and leaving little to no indication they had been there at all. Their speed and accuracy was what made them the best, always deployed on the highest top secret missions for the Allies. And while every mission was difficult and dangerous, none compared to this one. A single line in an intercepted German-coded message alluded to a secret munitions factory in Dresden. The mission had seemed straight forward, but all their usual tactics to obtain the information had failed. This mission was going to require a different approach.

"We could head to the base again, maybe there will be more soldier's there tonight we could try get in with…or maybe some of the women working in the Admin building?" Eddie offered.

"There was barely anyone there last night, I'm not sure there'd be many more tonight…." Nathan trailed off, the troops from earlier that day entering his thoughts again.

"Did you see her?" Eddie asked, swiftly changing the subject. Nathan's left eyebrow popped. "You know who I'm talking about." Eddie smiled. "The Golden Goddess. She walked past us today."

One thing that had become very clear in the short time they had been in Dresden, was that the Zwinger was the most talked about 'secret' among the troops, and it's Madame, the Golden Goddess, the most desirable thing about the city. Nathan had seen her. As he had the day before when they had gone to check for updates from the comms base that fronted as a bookstore for Allied communication. Head held high, shoulders back, dressed impeccably. It's hard not to stare at such breath-taking beauty as it strolls past, casting an air of insignificance to all around her.

"Gosh, what I wouldn't give to spend an hour looking at that." Eddie chuckled. "I'd do whatever she wanted. She could spend the entire time talking about paint drying and I wouldn't care, so long as I got to look into those pretty blue eyes." Eddie sipped his tea and stared at nothing, his mind clearly no longer in this room. "I bet she knows all kinds of stuff, all kinds of positions..." he trailed off.

Eddie's comment triggered a thought in Nathan's head. "Eddie, you're a genius."

"Was it ever a question?" His witty friend shot back.

"I bet she does know all kinds of things..." Nathan trailed off, the wheels turning in his head.

"You can get in line old chap! I saw her first, so if anyone is getting a minute of her time, it's me." Eddie replied, missing Nathan's point entirely.

"No, you git!" Nathan leaned closer. "Think about it. The one thing we know for sure is that the Zwinger is where all the men, especially the German soldiers, go every night, right?"

"Yeah." Eddie replied, still not following.

"Earlier today, when you were in the bookstore, I overheard some German troops talking about the Golden Goddess and they mentioned Richter."

"The Lieutenant General?"

"Yes. And if there is anyone who would know the location of a secret munitions factory, it would be-"

"The Lieutenant General!" Eddie started to catch on. "But how we going to get that info out of him?"

"Not out of him. Out of her. Apparently, the Lieutenant General and the Golden Goddess spend a lot of time together..." Nathan let the comment hang in the air, Eddie's face showing the signs he was finally getting on the same page.

"I bet she knows *all* kinds of things." Eddie smiled.

"Like the location of a secret underground munitions factory." Nathan winked.

THREE

The Zwinger

January 31st 1945, 9:16pm

The sounds of the Zwinger greeted any patron before the lights or aroma reached them. A beacon of light in an otherwise dreary street drew men like moths to a flame, eager to see, to taste, to touch. With its plush furnishing and lavish interior, the Zwinger wasn't just a place of promiscuity, it was a place where business deals were made, blackmail was rife and cigar smoke swirled around whispered secrets in dark corners. Within its walls, men were equalised, for it mattered not your profession or where you lived. If you had the cash, you could play.

Ava scanned the full, loud, boisterous room and smiled. She was proud of her establishment, regardless of the opinions of others or the dirty deals that went down between its walls. Lining up a row of shot glasses, she expertly poured the whisky, not spilling a drop.

"There you go, Dieter." She slid one of the glasses into the business mogul's hand.

"Danke, Ava." He threw the shot back and slammed the glass back down on the bar. "Another!" He demanded and Ava obliged, taking the man's money. This was his fourth shot, eagerly trying to forget a bad day or a bad year. 'Probably just trying to forget.' Ava thought and she couldn't blame him.

Something out of the corner of her eye caught her attention. "Here, have another." She slid the shot over to him. "Tilly, take these to the table up the back. I have to take care of something." Ava handed the tray of shots to Tilly as she moved towards the end of the bar slowly, fixated on Margot and the Councilman. The girls were tasked with teasing and toying with every patron to keep them drinking. Anything on top of garments was allowed, but if you wanted to play any further, you would have to pay. Margot was sitting on the Councilman's lap, giggling and lightly stroking the side of his face, no doubt whispering that he wasn't allowed to go any further with that hand of his. But the Councilman, who was several beers and a few shots in, was not playing by the rules and what started as a little game of pushing his hand away was turning into something more. Ava grabbed the bucket, not taking her eyes off Margot as she made her way around the bar, watching for the signal. The Councilman was becoming more aggressive, lifting Margot's skirts, pushing his luck. Margot quickly scanned the room, meeting Ava's eyes. She reached up and touched her left ear. That was all Ava needed. She moved quickly through the crowd, drawing the attention of her patrons as she passed, the regulars knowing what was about to happen and eager to watch the show. In a perfectly timed move, Margot rolled off the Councilman's lap as Ava doused him in ice cold water. Rage and shock quickly replaced the heat of his passion and he loudly cussed, standing to his feet, water pooling around his feet.

"What the hell was that for!!?" He bellowed, the attention of the entire room now on him.

"You know the drill, Norbert." Ava pushed back. "No pay, no play. Out you go!" Ava demanded, pointing to the door. Norbert looked about, realising he had the attention of the entire room.

He stepped closer to Ava, a full head taller than her and using it to his advantage. "I could have you shut down." He hissed low enough only for her to hear. She eyed him back. "Yes, you could. But then you would have to explain to your wife and three adult daughters how you even know about this place." He seemed unfazed by the threat of Ava's knowledge, as though he already had a satisfactory explanation for knowing about the Zwinger. "And then there's your mistress over the other side of town…" Ava left the sentence hanging in the air, its implied meaning clear between them. Norbert angrily picked up his coat.

"You've just lost yourself a patron." He seethed. Ava smiled. "I highly doubt that, Norbert. Now go home, sleep it off and I'll see you next week." She turned to leave, swinging back around. "And Norbert, the next time you want to play, cough up the money. You have enough of it." She turned, the eyes of the crowd all on her. Ava knew if she let Norbert walk out right now the embarrassment of the situation could do some damage and she didn't want to be on the wrong side of one of the Councilmen. The atmosphere needed to be lightened and his reputation maintained.

"Ladies and gentlemen, the Councilman has kindly offered to pay for the next round of beers!" She triumphantly yelled. The place erupted with cheers and the Councilman waved like the typical politician he was. Ava opened the door for him. "See you next week, Norbert." She gave him a wry smile, the steam from his ears almost visible as he made his way into the cold night air.

Ava chuckled as two men approaching the Zwinger caught her attention. She didn't recognise them, probably just some new troops in town, but something about them piqued her curiosity.

"Guten Abend, gentlemen." She flashed them her best smile. "Come to play?"

The men looked at her, little reaction showing on their faces. "Ja." They simply said and walked past her into the bar.

"Well come on in then…" She sarcastically muttered under breath.

January 31st 1945, 9:32pm

Nathan slid into the seat across from Eddie, scanning the room. The two looked at each other, saying nothing as they absorbed their surroundings, Nathan working double time to get his head in the game after walking past her. The scent of the Golden Goddess still lingered in his nostrils and as tantalising as the rose fragrance was, he needed to focus. He didn't know how he was going to get the information he needed, but he knew she was the key to getting it.

"Hallo boys!" A busty red head appeared, blocking Nathan's view of the room. "What will you drink?"

"Beer." Eddie replied, motioning with his hand to make that two. The busty red head seemed a little disappointed they were not more enamoured with her, but nodded and walked off towards the bar. Nathan watched her as she slid behind the bar and whispered something to the Golden Goddess who shot a glance in their direction. Nathan shifted his eyes away from hers, already aware they were on her radar.

"Any thoughts on where to find the book?" Eddie asked, using the code word they had agreed upon when referring to the information they needed.

"One." Nathan commented looking at his friend. Both dressed in Luftwaffe uniforms, they blended in with the crowd seamlessly. "But the night is just getting started." He followed, stealing another glance at the Golden Goddess, who was still looking in their direction.

January 31st 1945, 9:38pm

Ava kept an eye on the clock, each minute that ticked by dragged her closer and closer to Richter walking through the door. Pushing the uneasy feeling in her stomach aside, Ava finished pouring the beers for the two men who had just arrived and opted to take them over herself. She wanted to get to know her quietly mysterious new patrons a little better.

"So, who do we have here?" Ava smiled as she arrived at their table. Both men looked at her, expressionless. "You're going to have to tell me your names if you want your beers." She teased. Glancing at each other and back at Ava, they seemed to be weighing up whether or not the information was worth the price of a beer. Most men by now would have told her their first, middle and surname along with where they lived and how much money they made. These two seemed a little less eager, behaviour that made Ava suspicious.

"Rolf." The blonde-haired one finally confessed and motioned with his head to the other. "Werner."

"Well welcome to the Zwinger, Rolf and Werner." She lifted the beers. "Here is your beer. As it's your first time here, this round is on the house. You can set up a tab with Heinrich over there, our barman. Make sure you settle up before the end of the night or he will hunt you down." Eddie smiled. "Oh, I'm not joking." She responded. "But, unlike the beers," She leaned closer, expertly showing just enough cleavage to hopefully whet their appetite. "If you want to play, choose your girl." She motioned towards the ladies. "But you'll have to pay first." Ava smiled. "Now can I get you anything else?"

Rolf reached across the table and ran a finger down Ava's forearm. "How about some more of your time?" He asked. Ava smiled and leaned in closer, her chest purposely pressed against his arm. "Oh, dear Rolf," She cooed in his ear. "My time is already bought." She winked, motioning to a man who had just entered. "And I'm not sure you could afford me even if it wasn't." She kissed his cheek lightly. "Now, I'll get the girls to bring you some more beer when you're done with these." Ava turned to leave as Rolf grabbed her wrist.

"Two more question," He said as she turned back. "What's your name?"

She smiled, raising an eyebrow. "Well most men call me the Golden Goddess, but I'll let you call me Ava. Next question?"

"How did you know we had never been here before?" He asked.

Ava moved in closer again, meeting his gaze directly. "You can always tell who the fresh ones are because they never look you in the eye." Ava winked and removed her wrist from his grip. "Have a good evening, gentlemen." She smiled and turned on her heel, not waiting for a response. Certain their eyes remained fixed on her, Ava intentionally swayed her hips a little more as she walked away, her own gaze focussed on the man waiting at the bar for her.

"Guten Abend Lieutenant General Richter, the usual?" She asked, forcing a lightness to her tone that was always missing when she talked to this despicable man.

"Guten Abend my little kolibri." He responded, a lewd tone to his voice that made Ava's skin crawl. "Ja, the usual." He glanced at the clock making sure she caught the silent undertone of the look. He turned and walked to his favourite table where his two incredibly dim sidekicks had shooed away the patrons that were already seated. Ava began pouring the drinks, watching Richter pull out a cigar and light it up like he owned the joint. It wasn't the cigar that bothered her, rather it was the size of the man's ego that believed he did. Or at least owned her.

Ava placed the beer down on the table in front of the three men. "Hallo Ava, you are looking very beautiful tonight." Klaus, one of Richter's goons, reached out and tried to pull Ava onto his lap. Ava expertly spun out of his grip. "Uh-ah. Klaus, you know the rules. Besides, we both know you couldn't afford me." She strutted off, the sounds of laughter from Richter and his other goon, Hans, swallowed up by the crowd.

For the next 10 minutes Ava served her patrons with finesse, teasing and cracking jokes to keep them drinking more and having a good time. But as soon as the clock ticked 9:50pm she glanced in the direction of Richter. He stood and motioned ever so slightly with his head towards the back door. Ava nodded in response and finished up her conversation with the table of soldiers who had been drooling over her all night. Slipping through the crowd, she made her way out the back, pausing at the door and sucking in a deep breath, steadying herself. She hated this part.

Nathan continued to watch Ava as she moved about the bar. She was beautiful, there was no question, but it was the way she commanded the space that really drew him in. This was a woman who knew what she was about and Nathan found that kind of confidence mesmerising. He watched as Ava glanced up at the clock behind the bar and then in the direction of the man she had said owned her time. An unspoken exchanged between the two of them prompted the man to stand, Nathan recognised him immediately.

"Richter." He whispered, watching the Lieutenant General disappear out the back of the saloon, followed shortly by Ava. Maybe she wasn't lying about her time already being paid for. But why had they not gone upstairs? All the other women had. Something about this interaction was different and Nathan wanted to know what it was.

"I'll be back." He said. "If I haven't returned in 20 minutes, leave and never come back."

The snow crunched beneath her feet as she made her way towards Richter. He stood with his back to her, looking up at the sky, puffing away on his cigar, shrouded in the shadow of the fire escape. The sound of her footsteps drew his attention and he turned to face her, a sinister smile on his face that made Ava's skin crawl.

"Hallo my little kolibri." He touched the side of her face, the hunger in his eyes unnerved Ava. "You look particularly spectacular tonight." He said, cigar smoke dancing around his mouth.

"There's talk of the Gauletier visiting in the coming weeks." Ava replied, getting straight to the point, eager to get this over with.

"I knew that already." Richter puffed away on his cigar, a tone of discontent lacing his words.

"The Führer could be joining him." Ava continued. "He has apparently sent his people ahead of the visit, to get things in order."

"The Führer is coming?" Richter raised an eyebrow at her. "Who said this?"

"Margot heard Lord Mayor Neiland whispering to another government official." She looked up at Richter. "And later confirmed with me, after he'd been properly taken care of." She paused, letting the last part of her sentence land, knowing it would boil Richter's blood a little. His lust for her was always present at their interactions but he had never quenched his thirst. His discipline had surprised her at first, until she realised it was just a game. He wanted her to resist him to make the chase that much sweeter, the conquest more satisfying. Richter revelled in the knowledge he could have her at any moment it pleased him. It equally angered him knowing other men had. And yet, the game continued.

"They're apparently wanting to put together additional security detail for the Führer's city tour. They're looking for elite personnel to accompany the Führer." Ava continued, hoping to bring the exchange to an end quickly. She couldn't stand to be in his presence for longer than was needed.

"What else?" Richter pressed.

"That's it. Nothing more. We're done." Ava said and turned to head back inside. Richter grabbed her arm and swung her back, pushing her against the wall.

"We're done when I say we're done." He spat, spittle landing on Ava's face as Richter pinned her against the wall. "Now, what else do you know about this visit?" He demanded.

"Nothing." Ava said through gritted teeth. "I have no reason to keep anything from you." She glared back at him.

"I disagree, kolibri." Richter pressed his arm harder into her chest. "Don't forget I know what I know. It would take one word, filthy Jew, one word and you would be shovelling shit in a concentration camp by tomorrow afternoon. Untermensch." He spat the insult at her.

Ava's heart pounded in her chest, every inch of her wanting to lift a knee into his groin and run, but she knew better. She knew Richter. Ava forced her breathing to slow, to deepen. When her nerves had steadied, she lifted her eyes, locking in with Richter, softening her body against his.

"I promise you, I know nothing more," She whispered in a low, sultry tone. "But, if you let me, I will tell my girls to drop your name in the Lord Mayor's ear. He's looking for the best of the best to protect the Führer while he is here." At this Richter's countenance eased. "I can have them remind the Lord Mayor of how strong you are. How deeply dedicated you are to the Führer. That you would die for the Führer and for Germany." Ava watched as Richter's expression shifted. "Imagine being that close to the Führer. Imagine being able to tell him of your many conquests for Germany. Of the way you single-handedly progressed the war efforts in Germany's favour. Imagine if he invited you to permanently join his Cabinet because of your bravery?" Ava let the last question hang in the air, knowing it was the very thing Richter wanted most. More power. She could see him change before her eyes, each stroke of his ego reminding him of how useful she could be. Richter nodded, more drunk on the idea of power than the beer he had consumed.

"Very well then." He stepped back, releasing his grip on Ava and pulling out his little black book. He hurriedly made a note, slapping the book shut. "I want a spot on that security detail. Get it for me." He turned and marched back inside.

Ava let out a breath she hadn't realised she was holding. She straightened her outfit, chastising herself for letting her emotions get the better of her. That was close. He held the knowledge of her heritage over her like a noose, its promise of death a constant warning. But it wasn't death itself that kept her pandering to Richter's nightly rendeazvous. It was a threat much more powerful. Richter knew nothing of her family and Ava intended to keep it that way. For while ever she could keep Richter distracted with her, Ava's family could remain hidden in the walls of Dresden.

Shaking off the encounter, Ava pulled the top of her dress down enough to expose her cleavage, pushing away thoughts of her family and concentration camps. It was time to get back to work. Ava carefully made her way inside, eager to keep the men happy, completely missing the figure that had been hiding in the shadows the whole time.

FOUR

The Following Night

1st February, 6:43pm
To: Frankland
From: Secretary of State for Air, Sir Sinclair.
Subject: Operation Thunderclap
Agent Sinclair and Agent Flannagen report they
are close to locating secret munitions factory.
Have requested a few more days to confirm.

1st February, 9:26pm

"How are you going to get her alone?" Eddie sipped his beer, his voice low but eyes alert, scanning for wandering ears.

"Wait for an opportune moment." Nathan replied, keeping Ava in his peripherals as she worked the bar.

"And if one doesn't present itself?"

"Then we come back every night until one does." Nathan glanced at Ava, her quickly averting gaze taking him by surprise momentarily.

She had noticed them when they walked in but had sent the busty red-head over to them instead of coming herself.

"I still think that we should check the east-side of the city for the book." Eddie commented. "It makes the most sense and we both know time is of the essence." Nathan drew his attention back to his counterpart. Typical Eddie, eager to get in, complete the mission and get out. He was a great agent, one of the best, but his biggest struggle was patience. Eddie was more of a smash and grab guy, whereas Nathan preferred a more subtle, strategic approach. Together, they were some of the best Mi6 Agents in the field.

"Patience, old friend, patience. It makes more sense to narrow the search as much as possible rather than running all over the city trying to find the book." Nathan sipped his beer as the door to the saloon opened and the opportune moment he had been waiting for marched towards the bar.

Ava could see the steam already.

"Guten Abend Lieutenant General. Drink?"

"Ja." Richter replied curtly, clearly not in the mood for talking. Ava poured the shot of schnapps into the glass and watched as Richter snatched it from her and downed it.

"Another?"

Richter nodded. Ava poured the drink. He grabbed it, threw it back and slammed the shot glass back down on the bar.

"Outside. Now." He demanded and marched off, not waiting for Ava or even attempting to be discreet. Ava shot a glance at Heinrich who nodded his understanding and took over pouring the drinks. She wiped her hands and followed Richter outside.

"I'll be back." Nathan whispered.

"Where you going?"

"To take advantage of an opportune moment. Keep an eye on things here." Eddie nodded. Nathan slipped out from the booth and moved purposefully through the boisterous crowd, using its bustling presence as a distraction so he could slip out the back, unnoticed. Edging past the barman, he quietly made his way down the hall and up the first flight of stairs to the fire escape he had hidden in the night before. Silently easing himself out onto the metal scaffolding, he hunched low, tuning his ear to the conversation below.

"…that's all he said." Nathan heard Ava reply, watching the Lieutenant General pace back and forth, noticeably annoyed.

"That's it? That's all you have?" Richter spat back at her.

"Yes. That's all we've gathered tonight." Nathan was impressed with how measured Ava was keeping her tone. If she was intimidated by the Lieutenant General, it didn't show.

"What about the Führer? What more of his visit?" Richter demanded. This caught Nathan's attention. There had been nothing about Hitler travelling to Dresden in the intercepted comms.

"Nothing. The Lord Mayor hasn't been in tonight, nor any of the councilmen."

"Are you sure?"

"Of course I am sure." Ava's tone became defensive. "Do not presume I don't know how to do my job. If they don't come, I can't get you any information."

Richter stopped in front of Ava, the palm of his hand connecting with the side of her face with such force it echoed off the walls. It took everything in Nathan not to jump down from the fire escape and lay into the sordid excuse for a man.

"It would serve you well to remember that my lack of turning you in does not signify I have some need for you." He hissed at Ava who was cradling the side of her face. "You, like every other woman, are replaceable. Especially a Jewish one at that."

Surprise rippled through Nathan's mind as the weight of this revelation landed. He was starting to understand the arrangement that existed between the two of them, having only caught the last few seconds of their conversation the night before. It had been clear from that short interaction that Richter held something over Ava. Nathan now knew what it was.

Richter stepped back slightly. "Get me what I need, or next time my punishment will be more permanent." He reached out and tilted Ava's chin towards the light. "And we wouldn't want the Golden Goddess to be without her golden looks, now would we?" A sadistic smile crept across his lips as he traced his fingers down her neck, lingering where her exposed chest dipped beneath the plunging top. He leaned in close to her ear. "One of these days Ava, I will have you."

Nathan watched as Richter turned and marched back inside, leaving a trembling Ava still clutching her cheek. He paused for a moment, watching the woman below him, the shadows concealing her face. She was shaken but he was unable to tell how much. This was his chance. He moved swiftly, dropping from the fire escape to the snow below with a thud. Ava spun around at the sound, ready to fight for her life.

"It's ok, it's ok." Nathan quickly raised his hands, trying to communicate he meant no harm. "I don't want to hurt you."

"Captain Rolf, what are you doing here!?" Her eyes were wide and wild, anger seething from her.

"I just came to talk." He said, clearly not convincing her as Ava darted her eyes about, no doubt looking for the nearest escape route should she need it.

"You can't be back here!" She said through clenched teeth.

"I know, I just came to talk." Their eyes locked, tension palpable between them as they stood eyeing each other for a moment.

"I know." Nathan broke the silence first.

"You know what?" Ava asked sternly.

"I know who you are."

"And?" She shrugged.

"I know *what* you are." Nathan watched Ava's face shift as she realised what he meant. In an instant her demeanour changed. Squaring her shoulders back, Ava lifted her chin and rose to her full height.

"What's the price?" She looked down her nose at Nathan.

"What do you mean?"

"What's the price?" Ava stated her question again. "What must I pay for your silence? A night with the Golden Goddess? A night with every woman in there? What? What do you want?"

"Nothing."

"Nothing?"

"Well, something."

"Of course, you're a man."

"Not what you think."

Ava's left eyebrow lifted in question. "There is a line, even for common prostitutes, Captain Rolf."

"No. I don't want to sleep with you or any of your girls." Nathan clarified, uncomfortably.

Something shifted in Ava's face, like she suddenly understood what he meant. "Captain Rolf," she began to move towards him, swaying her hips in a mesmerising way. "Am I to understand that either you don't want sex," Ava placed her hand on his shoulder as she circled around him, tracing his shoulders. The sensation of her touch sent Nathan's heart into overdrive. "Or…that you don't want sex with me?" She stopped in front of him, the smell of her heady perfume clouding his mind. "Perhaps you would prefer Heinrich?" Ava's left eyebrow lifted in suggestive surprise.

"What? No!"

"We don't judge anyone's fantasies here at the Zwinger." She cooed.

"No, no. Look, listen," Nathan stepped back, needing some distance to clear his head. Her presence had a certain power over him that he found difficult to resist. "I don't want anything from you but some information. I'll keep my mouth shut if you can get me what I need to know." A stalemate of decision settled between them, puffs of warmed breath the only thing filling the space left at the end of his proposition. Nathan searched her eyes from a distance, unable to tell if she was leaning towards his offer or towards an escape. Even from this distance, her vivid blue eyes had a magnetic affect he found hard to resist. Any other place, any other time and he would not have resisted the urge pulsating in his fingers to reach for her.

Ava exhaled. "What information are you after Captain Rolf?"

The clang of trash cans echoed throughout the night, its twanging reverb echoing off the walls. Instinctively, Nathan stepped in front of Ava, scanning the ominous shadows for the threat, prepared to take on whatever danger emerged. Ava leaned forward, her breath warm against his neck. The sensation sent chills up and down his spine.

"Alley cat." She whispered and pointed to the tabby running off. "And I don't need your protection, Captain Rolf." Ava stepped out from behind him. "Much like that alley cat, I can take care of myself."

"I don't doubt it for a minute." Nathan turned to face Ava.

"Now what information do you need in exchange for your silence. The name of a politician's mistress? A list of things you can blackmail the Orpo with?"

"The location of the secret munitions factory and the Führer's travel itinerary for the next 3 weeks." Nathan cut to the chase.

A furrow formed in Ava's brow. "The Führer's itinerary will be easy enough, but there is no munitions factory in Dresden." Ava's tone changed, and Nathan couldn't sense if it was due to fear or the difficulty of his request. "And why do you need to know this?" Ava's eyes narrowed. "You're in the army, surely you could find out this information for yourself?"

"I could, but someone with your...expertise...would be able to find it faster." He replied. "I'd be willing to pay for it." A look of anger flashed across Ava's face. "Do you think by throwing money at me I'll just roll over and do what you ask?"

"I was hoping it might persuade you, yes." Nathan sighed, realizing he was losing her quickly. "I can assure you, Ava, we want the same thing. So if you can do this for me I will make it worth your while."

"And what's that?" She asked.

"What's what?"

"What is it that we both want?" Ava pressed.

Nathan paused, crafting the truth into a sentence that wouldn't give away who he really was. "The end of this godforsaken war."

"But Germany is…" Ava's voice trailed off ending in a loaded pause. Her eyes ran up and down his body, a scan he felt every inch of. He released a slow breath and with it the surge of desire the had filled his body under her gaze.

"You're a spy." Ava stated in a calm that was surprising to Nathan.

"Do I look like a spy?" He asked, motioning to his uniform and doing his best to dissuade where her thinking was going.

"You are dressed like a Nazi but you don't act like a Nazi." She stepped closer. "No real Nazi soldier would want this war to end. But every Jew…" She scanned his eyes, as though the truth could be found there. "And Allied soldier would." Satisfaction swept over Ava's face, clearly pleased with herself. Frustrated with her persistent hunt for truth, Nathan slid his hand under Ava's elbow and moved them both into the shadow of the fire escape. "Let's say I am what you think I am, would you help me?"

Ava's eyes were bright with the energy of a million questions swirling in her mind. Nathan waited for her to respond not wanting to rush her in case her loyalty to Germany was stronger than her Jewish heritage. This dance of trust was proving difficult to read.

"What will the Allies do with this information?"

"Use it to their advantage, of course." Nathan replied in a low, measured tone, keeping a vigilant on the backdoor to the Zwinger. "The war is being fought on many fronts, but if we are able to take out the munitions factory then we will be able to cripple Germany's war efforts quicker and hopefully bring an end to the mass genocide of your people." Nathan could see the wheels turning in Ava's mind as she looked away, staring off into the distance but with such certainty he almost turned to see what she looking at. Her intoxicating sapphire eyes flickered back to his with a clarity that stunned him.

"Can you get me and my family out of Germany?" Ava asked, barely above a whisper.

The backdoor to the Zwinger swung open with a bang as a very drunk Klaus, stumbled out into the snow. "Avaaaa!" He called, scanning the back alley. "Avvvvaaaaa!"

"I have to get back inside." Ava whispered, hurriedly picking up the skirt of her dress.

"What about the location." Nathan grabbed her arm.

"Avaaa! Ava!" Klaus continued to wail.

"I- I ah, I-"

"Ava! Are you here?"

"I have to go!" In one swift move, Ava pulled her arm from his grip and went to step into the light only to be stopped by a small red bird landing not far from their hiding spot. Ava and Nathan froze, eyes fixated on the little creature, willing it to not move for fear of it exposing their location. But just as quickly as it had arrived, it flew off, the movement catching the attention of Klaus. He began to trudge towards them.

"Ava! Is that you? Richter wants to see you…" Klaus slurred in their direction.

"Kiss me." Ava hissed.

"What?"

"Just kiss me!" Ava grabbed Nathan's lapel and pulled his lips to hers, using his body to shield both their identities.

"Oh, entschuldigung!" Nathan heard the soldier say. "Have you seen the Golden Goddess?" He demanded, undeterred by the romantic scene before him. Keeping his back firmly to Klaus, his lips firmly on Ava's, Nathan motioned toward the corner with his hand, trying to remain present when his mind and body wanted nothing more than to explore the body pressed against his own.

"Excellent. Guten abend." Satisfied with the answer, Klaus clumsily stumbled towards the direction Nathan had pointed. "Ava! Avaaa!" His voice trailed off as he rounded the corner, but the world had already gone silent for Nathan. He lingered for as long as he could on Ava's lips until she pushed him away. "I have to get back inside. But can you promise?"

"Promise what?" Nathan asked, still reeling from the kiss.

"Can you promise to get me and my family out of Germany if I get you the information?" She pleaded.

"Yes. Of course. I'll do whatever it takes." Nathan whispered. Ava stepped around him, making her way to the bottom of the fire escape. "I'll get you the information but you must leave. Now. And do not comeback until I have sent word." She began to ascend the stairs.

"How will I know you've sent word?" Nathan reached for her hand to stop her, wanting to reach for more than an answer. Ava turned and paused for a moment, formulating something in her mind.

"Be at the Martin Luther Monument every day, at midday. Wait for 15 minutes. If a small child does not show up wearing this pin," She pointed to a tiny bird pinned to her top. "Then leave and keep returning every day until the child shows. Now go!" She hissed.

"I can't, my partner's inside."

"I will send him out. But you must leave. We can't risk Richter getting suspicious and there is very little that gets past him. Go!"

Ava turned and made her way up the stairs. Nathan watched as she slipped into the building via the same window he had come out. He slowly turned and began to make his way through the shadows to the hideout, the taste of the Golden Goddess still lingering on his lips.

Ava watched from the fire escape window as Captain Rolf, if that was even his name, disappeared into the darkness. She released a low, slow breath, the events of the evening playing on repeat in her mind. The gravity of the task she had just committed to weighed in on her. It was dangerous. Incredibly dangerous. If Richter, or anyone, found out that she had agreed to feed Nazi secrets to an Allied spy she would not see the light of the next morning. Finding such information was not going to be easy, if the information was there to be found at all. But if she could do it, then maybe, just maybe, she could free herself and her family.

She instinctively ran her fingers over the Rosenfink pin attached to her top. When the Rosenfink had landed in the alley, she knew it meant something. It was the third one she had seen that day. To see one in a year would be lucky, but three in one day? That was significant.

Making her way downstairs into the bustling saloon, Ava scanned the room, looking for the Captain's partner. Richter was sitting at his usual spot, drinking beer but Ava's presence, as always, drew his attention. She could feel his eyes on her but did not meet his gaze, instead focusing on finding Margot who, as luck would have it, was getting comfortable with Captain Rolf's partner. Ava needed to get him out without making it seem suspicious and there was only one way she knew how to do that.

Reaching for the bucket, she made her way towards Werner. The crowd followed Ava's movements, knowing what was about to happen and hungry for the spectacle. She lifted the bucket high, dousing both Margot and Werner in the cold, wet liquid, shock rippling across their faces.

"Ava!!!" Margot yelled.

"That's it, Cadet, you've had enough. No pay, no play. Now get out." Ava motioned with her hand towards the door, shooting Margot an apologetic look. Margot stood up and moved out of the way as an angry Werner followed, grabbing his jacket and storming out of the saloon doors. Ava turned to face an eager crowd, hungry for more. So Ava did the only thing she knew they would respond to, even though the very act made her sick.

"Hail Hitler!" She threw her arm in the air and was met with the expected response of a loyal crowd. In that moment she looked out at their raised hands, feeling her conviction grow.

"Now! Let's drink!" She yelled and the crowd burst back into high spirits. Margot stormed passed Ava, shoving her shoulder, leaving a trail of wet footprints in her wake. Ava immediately followed her friend towards the kitchen, knowing she needed to do some damage control.

"What the hell was that for Ava? I gave you no signal that things were out of hand. I had it under control. And you didn't even give me a chance to get out of the way. What the hell Ava!?" Margot seethed between shivers.

"I did it for a good reason." Ava glanced behind her. Slipping her hand under Margot's arm, she ushered her into the pantry. "I'm sorry I threw water on you but I need your help." Ava whispered, her eyes constantly diverting to the pantry opening, ensuring they were alone. "I can't explain everything right now, but I need you to get some information for me." Ava pulled down a towel from the top shelf and handed it Margot.

"What kind of information?" Margot asked, wrapping the towel around herself.

"The kind that could end the war."

FIVE

The Little Black Book

2nd February 9:56pm

Colonel Hans Vogel and Colonel Klaus Stein stumbled into the saloon unaccompanied by their lord and master, Richter. The two buffoons generally began a rowdy round of Cerevis. A game in which you weren't allowed to refer to the cards as "cards" but rather as spoons, amongst other rules. Without fail, a round of Cerevis always ended in someone getting punched in the face over a dispute in points. Tonight was no different and Ava kept an eagle eye on the games proceedings. The more they drank, the more out of control the game became until the moment Ava had been waiting for. Klaus, in a fit of rage, stood and demanded a re-count because he was certain he had not called the cards "cards" but rather "spoons" and if he had called them cards then he would have remembered calling the cards "cards"! Back went the arm but before the fist could connect with Hans' nose, Hans jumped to his feet and planted a bulging fist on Klaus' mouth. The very drunk soldier fell head of toes, breaking the poker table behind him and sending the bar into a brawl.

Ava calmly made her way around the bar, climbed onto a stool and stepped onto the countertop. She stood surveying her brawling patrons. Placing two fingers in her mouth, she whistled loudly and stamped her foot three times. Like a herd of deer caught in headlights, the brawling crowd froze.

"Gentlemen! This is not how we behave at the Zwinger. Am I going to have to close up early tonight?" She threatened.

The crowd rumbled their protest.

"Alright, alright. If you can promise me you won't do it again, I'll keep the bar open." She smiled flirtatiously, swaying her hips on purpose as she moved along the bar top.

The crowd mumbled their promises.

"Good." She smiled, seductively leaning down to pick up a bottle of schnapps. "Now, who wants a shot!?" The crowd lurched towards her and the mood lifted as the schnapps poured freely.

Meanwhile, Margot had hurried to Klaus' aid. Out the corner of Ava's eye she saw her partner in sleuthing lead the bloodied and drunken man upstairs, promising to take real good care of him.

3rd February 1945, 8:33 am

To: Secretary of State for Air, Sir Sinclair.
From: Frankland

Subject: Re - Operation Thunderclap

Update Sinclair?

3rd February, 10:04am

"Nothing."

"What do you mean nothing?" Ava demanded.

"He knows nothing." Margot slumped back in her chair.

"How is that possible? He is always with Richter. He must know something." Ava protested knowing it was futile, Margot had done her best but Klaus was a useless as he appeared.

"I thought so too, but he said he has no idea if there is a secret munitions factory, he's not high ranking enough." Margot sipped her coffee.

"And you showed him a good time?" Ava asked, again knowing the question was futile. Aside from herself, Margot was the most sort after girl in the brothel, any man would happily give over the Führer himself and any strategic locations if it meant an evening with Margot.

"Of course I did! I've done less in the past and gotten more information out of a man than I did last night. I'm surprised you'd even ask." Margot sat back in her chair and sipped her coffee, slightly offended.

"I'm sorry, I don't mean anything by it. I just really need that information." Ava stared out the window, her mind scanning for a new plan to get the Allied spy what she had promised. She wasn't so worried about him releasing her identity, what did he stand to gain from that? What she was more fixated on was bringing this war to an end as fast as possible so that her, her family and her people could finally be free.

"There was one thing that Klaus said, but I don't think you're going to like it." Margot leaned forward.

"What is it?" Ava glanced back at her friend.

"Klaus made the comment *"that kind of information would be in Richter's black book though!"* Margot mocked, slurring her speech as she imitated the drunk German soldier. Ava slumped back in her chair and let out a sigh. She had hoped to avoid attempting to get the information from Richter directly. But, if a man who spent every waking moment with Richter didn't know if there was a secret munitions factory in Dresden, there was probably an even slimmer chance of a councilman knowing or a high-ranking politician being willing to give up the information. Her only option was to get her hands on that little black book.

"There's only one way to get that information." Ava finally spoke, realising what needed to be done, no matter how sick to the stomach it made her. A questioning furrow formed in Margot's brow.

"I'm going to have to give Richter the one thing he has always wanted."

"What's that?"

"Me."

3rd February, 11:32am

To: Agent Sinclair

From: Secretary of State for Air, Sir Sinclair.

Subject: Re - Operation Thunderclap

Frankland wants an update.

3rd February, 12:08pm

Nathan looked at his watch again. Another seven minutes and he would leave. Hopefully this time with the location of the munitions factory. High Command was getting impatient and he wasn't sure he could keep them from dropping the bombs before he had a chance to get them what they wanted, let alone figuring out how to get Ava and her family out of Dresden undetected and unharmed. He had been so swept up in the taste of her, that he hadn't thought about the level of difficulty surrounding what he had agreed to. Trying to remain undetected behind enemy lines was difficult enough. Smuggling a Jewish family out of Nazi Germany would be nearly impossible. That was assuming she meant a family in the traditional sense. Did she mean the girls at the brothel? Were they who she referred to as family? Or was she hiding a husband and children? And what husband would be ok with her profession? Maybe he was in a concentration camp? Was there a husband at all?

The questions continued to swirl on repeat as Nathan pretended to read the newspaper he had picked up. Sensationalised headlines made his blood boil. Goebbels was, unfortunately, exceptionally good at spinning a story so that the Nazi's believed they were doing the will of God.

'Where was God in all of this?'

The thought lingered in Nathan's mind like a pesky fly buzzing around that he couldn't swat. He knew that God was good, but the world that burned around him wrote a different truth. One of suffering and pain. Of destruction and death. And that was where the faith Nathan had, met its biggest challenge. How could a good God allow the annihilation of the people who served and loved Him? Like always, this question was met with silence and Nathan was presented with a choice to keep believing in a good God or to abandon the faith he had held since he was a child. Neither path seemed appealing right now. He released a sigh of surrender, unable to find an answer to the questions that plagued him, so there they remained, suspended in his thoughts.

Frustrated, Nathan closed the newspaper and looked at his watch. 12:16pm. Folding the paper, he stood and stretched his back. Maybe tomorrow she would send someone. He started to make his way back to the apartment, sending a quick prayer to heaven for Ava's safety. And the safety of her family. They were going to need it, because if Nathan couldn't find a way to get them out of Dresden soon, then they would be caught up in the impending bomb attack from Allied forces. And he wasn't sure even God would be able to save them.

3rd February, 4:11pm

Ava wrapped the towel tightly around her body, a shield from the cold both around her and within, and tip-toed to her room. The afternoon sun had poured itself all over her bed, the desire to curl up and soak in its rays too strong to resist. Ava lowered her body onto the soft, silky sheets, feeling the worries and pressure of the world slip away, if only for a moment. The sun's rays were just as fleeting as anything in this world and Ava was determined to enjoy them before they were lost to the night. Like she was.

A sigh escaped her lips, prompted by the thoughts of the evening ahead. The plan they had come up with was simple in execution, yet timing was everything. If anything tripped the flow of events, the consequences could be fatal. Everything hinged on Richter's little black book.

Ava would invite Richter up to her room for their usual chat, which she knew would be a surprise to him but with the right persuasion she was sure she could distract him from the abnormality. Once inside she would offer to take his jacket, knowing the little black book resided in its top left pocket. Instead of hanging the jacket up, Ava would place it outside her door. Margot would then take the jacket, find the book, locate the information and copy it out. Slipping the book back into the jacket pocket, she would carefully drop the jacket inside Ava's door, Richter none the wiser.

Ava stared at the dust particles dancing on drafts of air above her head, illuminated by the sun. A longing for simpler times when the world seemed full of light and love swelled within her but she pushed it aside as quickly as it had rose. There was no time for water coloured memories that were too fleeting to hold. Her focus needed to be on the task ahead. While Margot took care of extracting the information, Ava needed to take care of Richter.

A shiver went down Ava's spine. The last part was what unnerved her the most. Ava would have to work hard to hide her repulsion towards Richter. It would take every trick she had ever learned to not let the nausea at his touch seep out. Never in her entire career had Ava come across a man who made her feel this ill. The very idea of his body against hers made her skin crawl. But she was going to have to overcome it if she had any hope of getting the information she needed to get her family out of Nazi Germany.

"Out of Germany..." she whispered to no one.

Even if she managed to achieve that, what was for them beyond the city limits of Dresden or the borders of Germany? Her profession may transcend language, but she was established here. She was tethered to no one and that freedom was everything to Ava. It wasn't that she was lacking opportunity. Most nights she received a marriage proposal. If she had wanted to find a man to make an "honest" woman of her, she would have no problem. But something held her back. Something about being her own woman, about remaining single, kept her from taking the path that her sister had, that most women were expected to walk. Would that same liberty be available to her outside of Dresden?

Ava rolled off the bed, leaving unanswered questions swirling with the dust particles, her focus shifting to the part of the plan that was up to her to fulfil. A night with Richter. She would trade anything to not have that man's hands on her body. Until now, she had managed to keep Richter's appetite satisfied with the secrets she gathered each night. But tonight was different. She had nothing in her arsenal of information that would warrant a change in location for their nightly chat. Or did she?

Ava stared at the little Rosenfink pin, its shiny exterior glinting at her in the sun. Information really was power. Maybe she could satisfy Richter with something he desired only slightly more than her - powerful information. Ava picked up the pin, rubbing her thumb across the little red bird that stared back at her. The most powerful information she had at her disposal was the knowledge that there were two spies in Dresden, hunting for the secret munitions factory. And maybe that was the key she needed to keep Richter's hands off her and get her family out of Dresden.

SIX

The Piece of Paper

3 **rd February 9:38pm**

Richter stamped the snow off his boots at the door of the Zwinger. His was a presence felt before he had entered a room. The saloon quieted slightly as he stepped through the doors, Hans and Klaus bumbling around him to clear the idiots sitting at his table. Removing his gloves, he eased himself into the chair, expecting Ava to be pouring his beer already. She was absent from her usual post. Interesting. Klaus scurried off to get their drinks as Richter scanned the room, tipping his head to various influential figures who came here to drink away the outside world. Idiots. Did they not know that by being in this very room they were vulnerable? Exposing their deepest secrets for a few moments of ecstasy? His little hummingbird would see to that. Ava had proved to be an invaluable resource over the years and he had made every effort to keep blindly caged in the Zwinger. Let her think she is free and able to do as she pleased.

The atmosphere noticeably shifted in the room. A flash of red hovering at the top of the stairs caught Richter's attention, immediately mesmerising him. She descended the stairs seductively, the metronome movement of her hips amplified by the deep red of her dress. Richter recognised the dress immediately. He had bought it for her the day after they had first met. Back when he had momentarily been swept away by her and foolishly showered her with gifts in the hopes of winning her heart and having her forever. But Ava would not be swayed and Richter soon realised baubles and trinkets were nothing to her. Ava's playing hard to get infuriated him and yet fuelled his desire for her even more. What had started as infatuation had grown to an obsession but nothing he did, no amount of money he offered, would cause her to relent on her consistent answer of 'No.'

Then the tables turned in Richter's favour. The army was marching the Jews they had rounded up the night before out of the city, most still dressed in their nightgowns, barefoot and trudging through the snow. The streets were lined with German citizens, spitting and yelling at the dirty Jews. The scene had made Richter proud to be German as they purged the city.

Even though she had tried to blend in, Richter had noticed Ava in the crowd, watching the spectacle. Silent and still. Her face hidden by a large hat and expensive sunglasses. Completely caught up with fantasising about her, he had almost missed the moment that permanently changed the dynamic between them. A small child stumbled as she passed by Ava and to his surprise, Ava reached out, catching the child before she fell to the ground. As Ava set her on her feet again, she placed something in the girl's hand. Richter wasn't sure what it was until later that evening, when he beat the child until she gave up what Ava had given her. The small Jewish bible was like a red flag to a bull.

He had wasted no time sending Klaus and Hans to find out if Ava had even a drop of Jewish blood running through her veins. Just one Jewish grandparent listed in her heritage would classify her as a

Mischling and therefore a Jew, unless she had a German Blood Certificate. The result of their search had changed everything.

When Richter arrived at the Zwinger he had wasted no time, dragging Ava out to the alley and calling her out on what she really was. She had held her own, not showing any sign of fear when he told her what he had seen. Ava asked what he wanted in exchange for his silence. Assuming his response would be sex, she had pressed her body up against his, the sensation of her soft skin almost sending him over the edge. But Richter wanted more than just a few minutes of pleasure. He wanted it all. The power and the woman.

So instead of taking her right then and there, he promised to keep his mouth shut if she would open hers. He wanted the stories of unfaithful husbands and wives, political deals, any and all business trade, the whisperings of the elite, everything that he could use against those who ranked higher than him. Her shock at this being all he wanted was visible but she had complied ever since. Blackmail was a powerful motivator. He had kept his part of the deal and not told a soul about Ava's heritage. But it wouldn't be long. He was close, so close to getting what he wanted and then he could force Ava to marry him in exchange for his eternal silence. Until then, he had to control himself, even if seeing her in that dress drove him mad with lust.

Ava stopped right in front of him, pressing her body against his leg. Richter regulated his breathing, focusing not on the way her breasts teasingly poked above the bodice of the gown but on keeping a level head.

"Guten Abend, Lieutenant General." She cooed at him. "Can I get you a drink?"

"Ja." Richter responded flatly, maintaining his steely look in order to hide what the smell of her perfume was doing to him. Ava leaned down, close to his ear, the warmth of her breath and proximity causing Richter's pants to tighten.

"Why don't you come to my room and I'll pour you one there?" she whispered.

"Here is fine." He replied, doing all he could to remain focused. Ava leaned in closer.

"I have some important information that needs to be shared somewhere that prying eyes or eager ears can't be found." She straightened, giving Richter a knowing look. Ava had never invited him to her room before. If she was doing so now, then the information must be of great value. He held her gaze a few seconds longer, trying to read if she was telling the truth. If she was, then this could be the intel he'd been waiting for, the opportunity that would put him on the Führer's radar and into his cabinet. And he wanted that more than anything.

Richter nodded. "9:50pm."

Ava stared out the window. This had to work. It was going to work. She released a silent prayer, doubting anyone would be listening, some habits were hard to shake.

"Hallo my little Kolibri." Richter let himself into her room. Ava remained looking out the window, stilling the shudder that wanted to escape at the sound of his pet name for her. It was showtime.

"Hallo Richter." She turned and smiled, picking up the wine from the table beside her. "Drink?"

"Isn't that why you summoned me here?" Richter moved about her room, looking around, touching her things. Ava breathed deeply, calming the anger at his arrogance. "There have been many stories whispered among men of what this room holds. The colours. The heady fragrance. The pleasures, that can be found between these walls." Ava held the wine out to him as Richter walked past her. "I'm a little surprised Kolibri that it has taken this long for you to invite me into your room."

"Sometimes the safes place to share a secret is the place where many secrets are made and kept." She raised her glass towards him. "Prost."

"Prost." They both took a sip of wine. "You make a valid point my little Kolibri. So tell me, what's this little secret you have that's so important."

"Join me on the couch first." She sat on the chaise under the window, patting it gently, summoning him. Richter made his way over to her, removing his jacket as he came closer. Ava seized the opportunity. "Let me take that for you." She stood, taking the jacket and placing it over her arm. She put a hand on either shoulder and pressed gently, signalling for Richter to sit.

"You take a seat and I'll hang this up. We need more wine too. Make yourself comfortable." Ava offered a suggestive smile as she made her way to the door of her bedroom. Slipping behind the antique clothing divider she had positioned earlier that day to cover the door, Ava stepped out of her room, quietly closing the door behind her. She knelt down, exchanging the jacket for the bottle of wine Margot had left beside the door and counted to 20. Slipping back into the room, Ava clocked the time on her wall, starting a mental stopwatch in her head. She had 20 minutes of keeping Richter entertained, starting now.

"Now, where were we?"

Margot watched from the other end of the hallway as Ava placed the jacket on the floor and picked up the wine. She waited a moment, and when she was sure Ava had gone back into the room, Margot crept out, quickly and quietly making her way down the hall. Folding the jacket under her arm, she turned to head back when the sound of voices drawing closer froze her. There was no time to make it back to her room. Panic flooded her stomach as she frantically searched for a hiding place, the only option was the bathroom across from Ava's room. She hurriedly let herself into the bathroom, gently closing the door, missing the disrupters by seconds. She pressed her ear to the door. By the tone of the woman's voice, Margot could tell it was Tilly. Remaining completely still and hoping beyond hope that Tilly wasn't going to stop at the bathroom, Margot bit her lip and held her breath. If Tilly discovered her with Richter's jacket, she wasn't sure how she would explain it. No one knew of Ava's plan or the spies and Tilly's jealousy of Margot would see her waste no time in taking Margot out. The voices grew louder and just as quickly slipped away, passing by the bathroom. Margot let herself breath again. She waited to hear the click of Tilly's door and carefully cracked open the door. She scanned the hallway and once certain it was clear, she attempted again to get the jacket back to her room. Time was ticking.

"You were about to tell me what was so secretive that it couldn't possibly be shared anywhere else." Richter leaned back against the chaise, arms resting on the back of the couch and one leg across the other. The smug look on his face boiled Ava's blood.

"But first, let me top up your glass." Ava made her way over to the table beside him, picking up the bottle opener and resisting the urge to plough it into his neck. Richter reached out and grabbed her hand, pulling Ava down onto his lap.

"Why don't you just tell me what is so important so we can get onto more interesting topics…" He nuzzled her neck. Ava playfully pushed him away, escaping his hold.

"The information I have is likely to put you on the radar of high command, possibly make it all the way to the Führer." She let the last part of that sentence hang in the air like a piece of meat dangling in front of a hungry lion. Richter leaned forward, a spark present in his eyes. He had taken the bait.

"I'm listening."

"A few nights ago, two men walked into the saloon. I had never seen them before. Knowing that a new truck load of troops had arrived at the city that day I had assumed they were simply passing through. But then they returned the following night." Ava took a sip of wine, scanning Richter's face, pleased by the intrigue she found there. *'Yahweh, if you love my family at all, make this work.'* Ava silently prayed.

"One of the soldiers overheard our conversation in the alleyway, hence the different location." Richter nodded in acknowledgement. "He came to me after our conversation and, somewhat stupidly, told me what he was." Ava paused for affect and to draw out the time. Margot hopefully would have the jacket by now.

"What was he?" Richter prompted her, frustration seeping into his tone.

"An Allied spy."

"What!?" Richter stood, anger flooding his face as he began to move towards the door.

"Sit!" Ava demanded.

"Do not tell me what to do!" Richter bellowed.

"And let me finish." Ava stepped in front of him, grabbing his focus again. "There's more I need to tell you."

Richter sat down, his body visibly ready to jump into action as soon as Ava was done. She needed to draw this out for as long as she could, for all their sakes.

"He offered me protection in exchange for information."

"What kind of information?"

"A location."

"Of what."

"Of a munitions factory." Ava saw a muscle jerk in Richter's cheek. That was all the confirmation she needed.

"There is no munitions factory in Dresden. What did they look like?" Richter stood and Ava knew time was running out, he was too fired up to distract.

"Blonde hair, blue eyes."

"You've just described most of Germany!" Richter bellowed. "What were they wearing?"

"Plain clothes, they looked as though they were just normal German citizens."

"Would you recognise them if you saw them again?"

"Probably."

"What did you tell them?"

"I said I would get them the information they needed."

"What?" Richter's eyes flared again.

"I said that so I could buy some time and talk to you." She reasoned.

"Did you agree on how you were going to get the information to them?"

Ava nodded. "I told them to come back here every night and sit in the back left corner near the door until I passed them a note telling them to come to the alleyway."

"Did you see them enter tonight?" Richter demanded.

"Not yet, but they may have entered while we have been up here."

Richter paused, his eyes bright with fire, his rage shifting to an unnerving calm. A plan was forming in his mind. He looked at Ava, his hand brushing the side of her cheek tenderly.

"Well done, my little Kolibri." He turned and made his way to the door.

Margot stepped out of the bathroom and paused. She could hear raised voices coming from Ava's room and quickly arrived at the conclusion she didn't have much time. Closing the bathroom door again, Margot felt around for the book, her fingers finding it in his top right pocket. She pulled it out and immediately began to flick through, scanning each page. There were details of affairs and fraud, a list of what Margot could only assume were some sort of artillery and bits of writing that made no sense. Margot turned page after page, desperately searching when her eyes landed on a certain piece of information that ceased her page turning, a gasp of disbelief escaping her lips. For a brief moment, she considered abandoning the mission, the betrayal she felt was so strong. But then her eyes found what she had been searching for on the next page. There it was, the location of an underground munitions factory in Dresden. 'She has at least been honest about that' Margot reasoned, searching for something to write with when she heard Richter's voice bellowing from Ava's room again. They were running out of time.

In desperation, Margot tore the page out of the book and shoved it into her bra. Opening the door, she made her way to Ava's room, carefully opening the door and quickly placing the jacket on the ground.

"…Well done, my little Kolibri." Margot heard Richter say as she hurriedly shut the door and slipped back into the bathroom just in time to hear Ava's door open and Richter's heavy steps fade off down the hallway. Margot let out a breath and sucked another one in just as quick, trying to calm the adrenalin that was coursing through her veins. She turned and opened the door to the bathroom, pleading to whatever higher power existed that Richter wouldn't notice the missing page from his book.

"Margot!" Ava hissed from her door, motioning for her to come inside. Margot slid out from the bathroom and into Ava's room.

"Did you get it?"

"Yes." Margot responded, pulling the piece of paper from her bra and handing it to Ava.

"What's this?." Ava's eyes shot up.

"I ran out of time to copy it, so I just ripped the page from his book." Margot defended.

"He'll notice the page is missing!" Fear flooded Ava's heart. There was no way Richter wouldn't notice a missing page. Ava glanced at the clock. She needed to get back downstairs before Richter turned the saloon upside down looking for Allied spies that weren't there.

"I had no other option!" Margot justified.

"I'll figure something out. I need to get downstairs before Richter tares the place apart." Ava turned to leave.

"Wait!" Margot demanded, grabbing Ava's arm. "At what point were you going to tell me you're a Jew?"

Ava felt the colour drain from her face. "What do you mean?"

"Exactly what I said. When were you going to tell me you're a Jew?" Margot demanded again.

Ava removed her arm from Margot's grip. "Who told you?" Ava straightened.

"No one. I saw it in his book." Margot replied, anger filling her voice.

Ava took a breath. She had trusted Margot this far, surely she could trust her with this.

"I didn't want to implicate you. If you were ever asked if you were affiliated with the Jews I didn't want you to have to lie. So I kept it from you not because I couldn't trust you but because I wanted to protect you. All of you. You all rely on this place for safety, for money, for family and I didn't want to jeopardise that."

"Ava!" Richter called out.

Ava looked towards the door, shoving the piece of paper in her corset. "I'll explain everything later, but right now I need to go. Stay here until it is quiet again and then slip out. If he sees you in here, he'll know something is up." Ava made her way to the door, glancing back at Margot as she shut it behind her, unable to tell by the look on Margot's face if her secret was safe.

She hurried towards Richter, wanting to prevent him from going back to her room. "Will you keep your voice down!? My girls are working and do not need you distracting them."

"There are no men sitting at that table." Richter hissed at her.

"Then they must have come and gone while we have been up here." Ava motioned towards the stairs as she looped her arm through his, trying her best to distract him with the proximity of her body and a flirtatious tone. "For now, let's go downstairs, and if you give me some time, I will find you your spies." Richter stopped abruptly, pushing Ava up against the wall, his hand around her throat.

"Let's get one thing straight, my little Kolibri. You may have provided me important information but don't think for a second you are indispensable to me." Ava felt Richter's hand slid up her stomach, landing on her breast completely unaware he was cradling the missing piece of paper from his little black book.

"You have nothing that I can't get elsewhere. I don't need you. It is by my sheer grace I let you live. So you will find me those spies and if I discover you have been lying to me, I will waste no time taking what I want from you and throwing you to the pigs." Richter covered Ava's mouth with his, shoving his tongue inside. It took all Ava's strength to not gag at the invasion. As he pulled away, the piece of paper remaining undetected. Richter stepped back, a mixture of lust and anger on his face. He wiped his mouth with the back of his hand, removing the remnants of her lipstick.

"It would be in your best interest to make sure those spies are here tomorrow night." He threatened, as he turned and made his way downstairs.

SEVEN

The Hiding Place

4th February 10:52am

Ava stood at the doorway of the apartment block, unable to cross the threshold. There would be no turning back once she planted her foot on the other side. She had fervently searched for another option but every mental alleyway of possibility found its way back to this doorstep. If there was another way, she hadn't been able to find it. Reluctantly, she let herself in, her fingers finding the piece of paper and pin burning a hole in her pocket as she made her way upstairs. She still couldn't believe Margot had torn the paper out of the book. It was only a matter of time until Richter noticed the missing page and she was certain he would know it was her who had taken it, given what the scrap of paper contained. She could only hope that he wouldn't come looking for her until she had been able to get it to the spies. Then, at the very least, she could exchange it for the lives of her family and hopefully get them out of Dresden for good.

She let herself in and was greeted with a big smile and the fragrance of something yummy baking.

"Something smells good." Ava commented as she locked the door behind her.

"Just baking some bread. How are you my sister?" Ayala asked, her eyes shining. It amazed Ava how her sister, even in such dark times, could still somehow have a lightness about her. Despite the pain of her husband missing and her freedom restricted, Ayala to always have a sense of joy about her that made Ava's heart ache, longing for such joy.

"I am well. I can't stay long, I just popped by to ask Joseph something." Ava tried to keep her tone light, but the frown forming on Ayala's face told her she hadn't been successful.

"What is it sister? You seem troubled."

"Nothing, Ayala, I am fine. Just a little tired. Can I speak with Joseph?"

Ayala paused, unconvinced. "Joseph! Your Tanté wants to see you." Ayala called out. "You should take a break, come stay with us for a couple of days. Get some rest."

"Hallo Tanté." Joseph greeted her. Ava was sure he had grown a foot taller since her last visit.

"Hallo my boy. I need to borrow you for a short while, will you come with me?"

"Wait Hadar, you're taking him outside?" Ayala stepped in front of Joseph like a mother lion protecting her cub.

"Joseph?" Ava looked passed her sister. "Could you give your Mama and me a moment, please?" Joseph turned and made his way back to the lounge room as Ava took her sister's hand and led her into the kitchen.

"Ayala, I need Joseph's help." Ava whispered. "I need him to deliver a piece of paper to a friend of mine."

"Why can't you do it?" Ayala demanded.

"Because I will draw too much attention and no one must know about the information I need to get to my friend." Ava reasoned.

"I'll do it then. I don't want to send my son outside, no matter how much he can blend in."

"You will draw too much attention, Ayala, or worse be captured and I want to avoid that at all costs. Joseph, dressed in this, will look like any other little German boy and no one will pay any attention to him." Ava opened the package she had tucked under her arm to reveal a Hitler Youth uniform.

Ayala looked up at Ava, defiance still in her eyes. "Nein!"

"Ayala, if I don't get this information to my friend then everything I have done until this point is worthless and you will be putting me in a grave by the end of the week."

Ayala's eyes grew wide, fear written across her face. "What do you mean? What have you done?"

"The less you know the better." Ava whispered back.

"The less I know the better, yet you'll send my son outside like a lamb to the slaughter?" Ayala hissed back.

"I need you to trust me Ayala. Let Joseph do this one thing for me and I promise I will get him back to you. He will be no longer than thirty minutes." Ava pleaded, hoping Ayala would trust her and not see the fear that was swelling inside of her. Ava sighed. "Ayala, if Joseph does this, there's a chance I can get you out of Germany."

"What?" Ayala asked, barely above a whisper.

"There's a chance I could get you all out of Germany safely, but I need you to trust me and not ask for any more details." Ava repeated, hoping the promise of freedom would remove the last barrier that stood between her and her nephew.

Ayala stared back at Ava, her face giving nothing away. "Are you sure?" She finally whispered.

"Yes." Ava said with as much belief as she could muster. "Thirty minutes, sister, it's all I'm asking."

Ayala looked into Ava's eyes for a few seconds, searching for certainty. Something in the silent exchange between them shifted and Ayala reached for the package under Ava's arm, making her way into the lounge room.

"Joseph?"

"Yes, Mama?"

"Put this on. Your Tanté has an errand for you."

Joseph emerged from his bedroom, dressed in the uniform Tanté had brought for him. He didn't like how it felt or what it represented, but if it meant he was allowed outside even for a moment he would take the opportunity. Tanté and Mama turned and looked at him, worry in their eyes.

"You look perfect, mein Liebchen." Tanté said. "Ok, we need to go now. Ayala, we will be back soon." Tanté put her hand on Joseph's shoulder but Ayala stopped her, engulfing Joseph in a hug so tight he almost lost his breath. "Mama!" Joseph protested again. "I can't breathe!" She stepped back, her eyes a little wet. He smiled, hoping to put his mother's mind at rest. "Hurry back. Ok?" Mama directed her question to Ava, who nodded in reply.

"Let's go."

Joseph followed Tanté Ava down the stairs and out onto the street. They turned right and made their way down an alley, turning left, then right again. Tanté stopped, pressing them both up against the wall as a Nazi truck drove past. She turned to face him.

"Now, listen carefully Joseph." She said, reaching into her pocket. "Take this note, don't open or read it at all, you understand?" He nodded. "Good. Take this note down to the Martin Luther Monument. There will be a man waiting there with blonde hair and blue eyes and dressed like a Luftwaffe pilot. Hand him this note and then go straight home. Say nothing to him. Not a word you understand?" Joseph nodded again. "Use the back alleys to get down to the monument and if you see a soldier or Nazi official make sure you hail, ok?"

"Yes Tanté." Joseph replied, trying to ignore the worry that was growing in his stomach. Ava looked at her watch. "Are you not coming with me Tanté?" He asked, a flood of panic coursing through his body.

"I can't mein Liebchen. People will recognise me. You, however, are like a fox, cunning and smart, able to blend in and sneak around, undetected." She smiled at him. Looking deep into his eyes she paused for a second, as though trying to make a decision. "There's an old hotel up on the hill, across from the big gardens. You know the gardens I'm talking about?"

"Ja." Joseph nodded.

"Good. The hotel is called The Zwinger. It has red bricks and a balcony, and big red curtains in the windows. If you get in trouble or feel unsafe or scared, you run as fast as you can to that hotel, ok? I will be there." Joseph nodded in response as Ava looked at her watch again.

"Ok, my boy, you need to leave now or otherwise the man would have left and we will need to try again tomorrow." She wrapped her arms around him, tighter than normal. "Oh, I almost forgot." Ava pulled a small Rosenfink pin out of her pocket and pinned it to his uniform.

"That is a girl's brooch!" Joseph protested.

"You need to wear it Joseph, otherwise the man won't know who you are." She stepped back. "Ok, go now. Quickly." And with that, he was off, relishing the freedom of being outside and the feeling that he was on an important mission.

Ava watched as Joseph ran off down the street, offering up a silent prayer, hoping beyond hope that she hadn't just sent a lamb to slaughter.

4th February, 8:06am

From: Secretary of State for Air, Sir Sinclair.

To: Agent Sinclair

Subject: UREGNT - Operation Thunderclap.

Operation Thunderclap proceeding without location of munitions factory. Frankland wants to move, now. Pull out of current mission and report to Allied HQ.

4th February, 8:56am

. . .

From: Agent Sinclair.

To: Secretary of State for Air, Sir Sinclair.

Subject: Re - UREGNT - Operation Thunderclap.

Hold on execution of Operation Thunderclap for another 48 hours. Positive to receive intel within the day. Will send A.S.A.P. Civilians lives spared if we can concentrate attack on munitions factory and communication towers. We're close, Sir.

4th February, 12:04pm

Nathan sat down, paper in hand, agitated. If she didn't show up today with the information he needed, he would go to the Zwinger tonight to find out what was taking her so long. Time was running out. They had received word only that morning that the attack on Dresden was imminent. He had sent an urgent message back to Britain to hold off a few days longer so that he could find the munitions factory. It would still take a full 24 hours before that message was received and a further 48 hours before he had confirmation they weren't going to strike just yet. Hopefully he had bought him, and Ava, another 3 days to get the information.

He glanced at his watch. "Come on, Ava." He whispered under his breath.

"What if she doesn't come?" Eddie said in a low tone as he puffed on a cigarette.

"She'll come." Nathan replied, hoping he sounded more convinced than what he felt.

He returned is attention to the kids joyfully playing with a tattered soccer ball in the street, as though they weren't at risk of their lives being blown to pieces. It was moments like this that made Nathan wonder at the madness of life. How could there be such joy in the midst of such pain and death? He would never understand the paradox. All he could do was trust in a God that was bigger and more powerful than he was.

Nathan felt a tug on his sleeve, drawing his attention from the game of football. A young Hitler Youth stood before him.

"Verreisen." Nathan said, turning his attention back to his paper, hoping the kid would take the hint and leave. But the boy tugged again, harder this time.

"What?" Nathan said annoyed. It was then he noticed the pin. The boy handed him a white piece of paper. Nathan took the paper and opened up. Shock flooded his body as he stared at the location of the munitions factory.

"Is it?" Eddie asked, peering over Nathan's shoulder.

"It is." Nathan looked back up at the boy who nodded and turned to leave. As he did, the boy ran straight into a German soldier, almost knocking him over.

"Watch out, stupid boy!" The soldier barked, causing him to cower at the aggressive tone. Nathan recognised the soldier from the Zwinger. He stood up, calmly placing the piece of paper in his pocket, watching the German soldier begin to circle the boy.

"What's your name boy?"

"Dieter." The boy replied in a think German accent.

"Are you blind, Dieter?" Klaus asked.

"Nein."

"Are you hard of hearing?"

"Nein."

"Are you stupid?"

"Nein."

"Then why are you so incompetent as to run into me!?" Klaus yelled in the boy's face.

Dieter remained quiet and stared straight ahead.

"Are you now mute, boy?" Klaus demanded.

"Nein."

"Then you will answer my questions!" Klaus raised his hand, readying to hit the boy. Nathan instinctively stepped in and grabbed the man's arm before it could connect with the boy's face.

"Wait!" Anger flooded the soldier's face as he jerked his arm out of Nathan's grip.

"How dare you interrupt!" Klaus bellowed.

"Apologies Colonel." Nathan moved between the boy and the Colonel, pushing the boy behind him. "It's just I was about to reprimand the boy myself for being disrespectful. He needs to be disciplined and your time is too important to waste on this pesky child." Nathan watched as Klaus appeared to take the bait.

"My time is valuable." Klaus agreed. "Just make sure he is severely punished." He demanded.

"Ok." Nathan replied, unconsciously lifting his hand and signalling 'ok' with his fingers. He turned to face Dieter but froze at the sound of a trigger clicking behind his head. Nathan silently cussed to himself, realising he may have just blown their cover completely.

"What did you just do, Captain?" Klaus asked.

Nathan turned slowly, the barrel of a gun greeting him.

"What did you just do, Captain?" Klaus stated his question again, looking like a cat who had just caught a mouse. Nathan knew there was no returning from what he had done. He had to think quick.

"Hail Hitler!" He yelled, raising his right arm, the salute distracting Klaus long enough for Nathan to drop a shoulder into the man's stomach and knock him to the ground, disarming him in the process.

"RUN!" he yelled to Dieter and Eddie, who took off down the adjoining street, Nathan hot on their heels.

"Schnappt Sie!!" Klause yelled and the sound of chasing feet could be heard as Nathan rounded the corner to see Eddie and the boy pausing.

"Don't stop!" Nathan yelled, urging the two on.

"Follow me!" The boy took off and with no hesitation Eddie and Nathan followed him down alleyways, ducking left and right, weaving in and out of side streets and cobbled laneways. Nathan had lost all sense of direction when suddenly at the end of an alleyway the three of them spilled out in front of the Zwinger.

"Quick, this way!" The boy urged, the sound of the soldier's heavy boots getting louder. Nathan and Eddie followed the boy down the alleyway he had met Ava in and into the back entrance. They burst through the door to the surprise of Ava who was sitting at the kitchen table.

"Tanté!" The boy yelled.

"Joseph!" Ava stood and embraced the child, looking up at Nathan and Eddie in shock. "What is going on? What are you doing here?"

"The Nazis are chasing us. We need to hide!" Joseph frantically explained, the sound of the soldiers yelling and knocking on doors validating his explanation.

"Come with me." She said, grabbing Joseph's hand and leading them up the stairs. Rushing them down the hallway, Ava opened an oddly shaped door, revealing what appeared to be a storage closet.

"Ava, this won't do. If they search for us, they'll find us." Nathan whispered. Ava didn't acknowledge his comment, as she moved buckets and boxes to the side then pressed on the wall at the back. The wall panel swung open to reveal a secret door. Ava reached down her top and pulled out a long chain with a key on the end. She unlocked the door and held it open.

"Get in." She said, shoving Joseph through the door. Eddie wasted no time in following suit. Nathan paused at the opening.

"I'm sorr-"

There was a loud bang on the back door.

"Get in!" Ava's eyes flared at Nathan who quickly ducked under the door frame. "Do not make a sound. I will come back and let you out when it's safe." Ava shut the door to the tiny space, plunging it into darkness. The two men and the boy sat in silence.

Ava took a breath and turned quickly on her heel. She didn't know what had gone wrong or why they had ended up here, but now was not the time.

"Ava! Avaaaa!" She heard Klaus' demanding voice ring out. Steadying her nerves, she made her way downstairs, opening the back door to the kitchen.

"Klaus, what do you want? My girls are resting and you are going to wake them up with all this noise!"

Klaus went to step around her into the kitchen but Ava moved her body to stop him. "What do you want, Klaus?" She repeated in a measured tone, standing her ground.

"We are in pursuit of two men and a boy wanted for questioning. They were last seen on this street. I need to search the premises." Klaus, again, went to step inside. Ava didn't move.

"And as I said, my girls are resting and do not need to be disturbed. If such men had entered my premises, do you not think I would know about it?" Ava glared at him, both of them daring the other to try their patience a little further. "I don't know if it is the people you are looking for, but I heard footsteps a few moments ago going up the alleyway towards the field. Perhaps it was them." Ava did not take her eyes off Klaus, praying it was a convincing performance.

"She's right." A voice came from behind Ava caused both her and Klaus to turn in its direction. Margot was standing there, scantily dressed. "My room faces towards the field and I just saw two men and a boy running across the field towards the woods."

Klaus looked between them as Ava stood her ground, silently willing him to take the lie.

"Check the field." A low, familiar voice cut through the fragile silence. Ava looked over Klaus' shoulder to confirm the face that matched the voice. Richter stared back at her. Klaus shot an angry, distrusting look at both Ava and Margot and begrudgingly headed in the direction of the field. Richter stepped up towards Ava, leaning in close to her ear.

"If I find that you have been lying, my little kolibri, I will waste no time making good on my promise." He breathed her in deeply and released a low, hungry sound that made Ava cringe inside. He turned to follow Klaus, pausing at the bottom of the stairs. "Oh and Ava, cancel the reservations for your guests who often sit in the back left corner. Something tells me they won't be needing it tonight." He shot Ava a knowing look before turning on his heel and heading down the alleyway.

Ava waited until his footsteps had disappeared before she shut the door and found a furious Margot waiting for her.

"Margot, would you like a cup of coffee or -"

"Who are the men you are hiding in the closet?" She demanded.

Ava grabbed Margot's elbow and ushered her into the pantry. "Keep your voice down." She whispered sternly.

"Oh that's rich coming from you, Ava. If that is even your real name. You have been lying to me this whole time." Margot fumed.

"If you will be quiet for a moment, I will tell you everything." Ava glanced over Margot's shoulder, making sure no one was in earshot. "The two men are British spies and the boy is my nephew." Margot's eyes grew wide with a mixture of shock and anger. "They are the ones who need the information about the munitions factory. I sent Joseph to give them the piece of paper, knowing he would be able to blend in and go undetected. But something has gone wrong and they've ended up here."

"You have a nephew!?"

"Yes. He lives with my mother, sister and his younger brother in an apartment a few blocks from here that I keep them hidden in. If anyone knew that they were there, I would lose them forever. Margot, I need you to promise me you won't tell anyone." Ava pleaded.

"How have they not been discovered?" Margot asked, confused.

"By the grace of God." Ava responded, unsure why she had chosen those words. "We are German, all of us born here. We just also happen to be Jewish." Ava searched Margot's eyes, desperately hoping she wasn't making a huge mistake. "Margot, you need to understand, my lying to you has nothing to do with you and everything to do with protecting myself and my family. If there is a chance to finally get my family to safety, I would do anything to make that happen."

"Who else knows that you're a Jew, other than Richter?" Margot asked.

"The spies and now you. That's it." Ava swallowed the lump forming in her throat. If there was anyone Ava thought she could trust it was Margot. A silence fell between them, heavy with uncertainty, as Ava waited to see if she was right.

"What's your next move?" Margot asked, a hint of a smile forming on her lips.

EIGHT

The Closet

4th **February 1:13pm**

The door clicked opened, light causing her nephew and the two spies to blink away the shock of light.

"Finally." Werner said. Rolf hit Werner at his inconsiderate comment.

"Out. All of you." Ava demanded. The three of them crawled out of the closet. "Right, who is going to tell me what the hell happened?" Ava stood, arms crossed and unimpressed.

"Sorry, Tanté, it's all my fault." Joseph lowered his head. "I gave the man the piece of paper but I ran into a Nazi soldier. I made him angry and he stepped in and distracted the man." Joseph pointed towards Captain Rolf. "And then we ran."

Ava lowered herself to Joseph's eye level. "Mein Liebchen, are you ok?"

"Ja, Tanté, it was a great adventure!" He smiled as only a boy could, not really understanding the danger he was now in. Ava released a small sigh of gratitude. Maybe it was better that way.

"Thank you, Captain Rolf, for helping my nephew." Ava placed her arms around Joseph's shoulders and drew him close.

"You're welcome, and it's Nathan." Ava looked at him confused. "My name is actually Nathan. Rolf is my fake identity." He clarified. "And this is Eddie."

"Fake identity? Are you a spy? No wonder you called him an asshole." Joseph blurted out.

"You called a Nazi an asshole? And Joseph, watch your language." Ava reprimanded.

"I didn't call him an asshole." Nathan defended.

"Ja. When you did this." Joseph held up his hand, his index finger touching his thumb to form a circle.

Nathan sighed, rubbing the back if his neck. "In England, that sign means 'OK'." Nathan explained. "And I instinctively did it while I was trying to save your nephew from a beating."

"It's true, Tanté." Joseph defended. Ava released a conceding sigh. "Well, what's done is done now. But you have managed to anger a somewhat influential Colonel." Ava shook her head.

"Are you really a spy?" Joseph pressed again.

A smile spread across Nathan's face that caused the slightest flutter in Ava's chest, catching her off-guard. As quickly as it had surfaced, she pushed it aside. Nathan lowered himself to Joseph's height. "We' may or may not go on secret missions to find out certain things." Nathan teased, the sparkle in his eye matching that in Joseph's. "How about this, I'll teach you the secret spy handshake if you promise to not tell a soul about Eddie and me?"

Joseph eagerly nodded. Nathan held out his hand, using his free hand to manoeuvre Joseph's in a series of actions that Ava was sure were made up, but the delight on her nephew's face warmed her. The secret handshake ended in a high five.

"Our little secret." Nathan winked at Joseph.

"Is there anything else I should know about you? Other than your real name?" Ava asked.

"A lot, but nothing that matters right now." Nathan looked at Ava. She hadn't noticed how dark his eyes were when they had spoken in the back alley. "We need to get this information to our Commander." Nathan pulled the piece of paper out of his pocket.

"How do you plan to do that?"

"I can't tell you. But we need to get going."

"You can't leave. Half of the German army will be out looking for you if they aren't already. As I said, you angered the wrong soldier."

"Wouldn't be the first time." Eddie retorted.

"Ava, you need to let us go." Nathan responded, the urgency in his voice evident.

"It's too dangerous to stay in Dresden." Ava replied. "Richter will be looking for you and if he finds you in possession of that piece of paper, you'll be dead before the sun has gone down." Margot commented more bluntly than Ava would have liked in the presence of her nephew.

"Margot, could you take Joseph home please?" Ava glared at Margot who responded with a roll of her eyes.

"Nein, Tanté! I want to stay!." Joseph pleaded.

"Mein lamm, you have been so brave today and I'm so proud of you, but you are not safe here. I need you to sneak back home and not breathe a word of this to your Mama, you understand? Not a word. She will already be having conniptions that you are not home yet. Tell her you got lost on your way home. Hopefully she will believe you." Joseph nodded slowly as Ava unpinned the Rosenfink brooch from his lapel. "Come on, Joseph." Margot put her hand on the boys' shoulder. "You can fill me in on all your Tanté's family secrets." Margot mockingly taunted as she took Joseph from the room. Ava waited for the door to close, saying a silent prayer to whoever was listening to keep her nephew safe.

"Is there anyway to get out of Dresden undetected?" Eddie asked, drawing Ava's attention back to the issue at hand. She bit her bottom lip, contemplating all possibilities.

"I might have an idea." She slowly replied, a plan taking shape in her mind. "You'll need to remain locked in here until the evening. I can't run the risk of the other girls finding out you're here. For now, I need to go and make arrangements."

"What arrangements?" Nathan asked, pausing before climbing back into the closet.

"Capt- Nathan, you're just going to have to trust me." Ava replied. "I will get you out, I just need a little time." Nathan stared into Ava's eyes, clearly contemplating if he was willing to trust her. "Have I given you a reason thus far to not trust me?" Ava asked earnestly.

"No."

"Than trust me again, Nathan. I will get you out of Dresden so you can get that piece of paper into the hands of the people who can bring this godforsaken war to an end." Nathan held Ava's gaze a few seconds longer and then nodded slightly. He turned and ducked his head, as he made his way into the closet. Ava closed the door on them, locking it before she left, hoping that the crazy idea that had floated into her head was going to work.

❖

4th February 2:25pm

Richter lifted his foot to his knee, striking the match against his boot. He puffed deeply on the cigar, allowing the haze to surround him as he watched the two bumbling idiots before him make their way through the sludge, trying to find any sign of the spies. He was increasingly getting the feeling that the search was futile.

The spies hadn't run off into the woods, as Ava had said. But what would give her, and the other slut, cause to lie? Something about it wasn't sitting right.

What was the other slut's name? Maggie? Margaret? He nestled the cigar between his teeth as he reached for his little black book. Surely there was something about her in here. Thumbing the pages, he shifted through affairs and bastard children, blackmail and corrupt dealings, secret locations and -

Richter stopped.

At the bottom of the spread before him was the smallest tuff of paper, remnants of what had been there before. And what had been there before was the very information Ava had said the spies were seeking.

Richter drew a deep drag of the cigar, his mind swirling like the smoke around him and his blood boiling to match. This was no accident. There had been no missing page yesterday. Yet the day after he had been in Ava's room, there suddenly was. He let out a piercing whistle, grabbing the attention of Hans and Klaus.

"Come!" He yelled, turning on his heel and making his way back towards the road.

"Where are we going now Lieutenant General?" Hans panted beside him like a loyal dog.

"Bird watching." Richter replied, as he picked up his pace.

NINE

The Garbage Run

4 **th February 5:25pm**

Ava watched the clock as the hands drew closer to 5pm. She wiped the counter for the fiftieth time and she offered yet another plea for help to Yahweh, something that felt foreign and familiar all at the same time. Over the years her faith had dissipated, a concoction of shame, anger and disappointment building a barrier between her and Yahweh. If he truly was the Father he claimed to be, then why hadn't he prevented the death of her father? Why hadn't he kept Ayala's husband safe? Why had he allowed Hitler to torture and kill his people? If he loved us so much, why would he allow it?

Silence, as always, was the response.

Ava let out a heavy sigh. She was angry with Yahweh, she had been for years but no matter how much she fought against thoughts about him or tried to deny him, she had found his presence always lingered. Like an unsummoned distant memory that would appear, too hazy to fully grasp but powerful enough to command your attention. It was often in the insignificant moments, he appeared.

Like when her nephews smiled. The smell of fresh coffee. The Rosenfink landing on the windowsill.

Ava reached into her pocket and pulled out the pin, fastening it to her top. Thank God Joseph had not been hurt or taken. For that she would be forever grateful. But that was where the gratitude and the thoughts of Yahweh stopped. Her trust and belief that he cared for her had been destroyed long ago.

The door to the Zwinger swung open as Otto ambled on in. Right on time.

"Hallo, Otto." Ava called out as he quietly closed the door. He was a portly man, balding on top and always in a shirt that had seen better days. But for all the ways Otto lacked what the world would classify as beautiful or handsome, his heart was pure gold. Over the years he had become a friend more than a patron, helping Ava out with odd jobs as she needed. Hopefully tonight would be no different.

"Hallo Ava, how are you today?" He smiled as he sat down, taking the beer Ava had poured for him.

"I am well. And you?"

"A little weary but otherwise I am fine." He sipped his beer. "Is Olga about today?" He asked, a small smile forming at the corner of his lips.

"Yes, I'll go get her but before I do, I have a favour to ask." Ava leaned closer. "I need you to take out some extra to trash tonight." Otto held Ava's gaze, a flicker of confusion crossing his face.

"What kind of garbage?" He asked.

"Two big bags. They will need to be taken directly to the town dump."

"What's in them?"

"It's best you know as little as possible, but I will tell you this. The garbage is so old that it just might grow legs and walk out the door." Ava winked.

Otto paused, clearly weighing things up in his mind.

"Normally Ava, I start my run in the middle of the city and work my way out. Yours is one of my last stops. But tonight, I think I'll start on the outskirts and work my way in." He took a sip of beer. "Make sure the garbage is ready to go in 30 minutes when I leave to start my run. I'll take it as far as the edge of the forest just before the town dump. I'll knock three times on the wall and wait 5 minutes. If the garbage hasn't grown legs by then, I cannot be held responsible for anything that happens to it."

Ava nodded her understanding. "I'll get Olga." Ava smiled and made her way to the stairs. "Otto?" She turned back towards him.

"Ja?"

"Danke. For everything."

Otto nodded in response, quietly lifting the beer to his lips.

4th February 1945 5:42pm

Ava waited for Olga's footsteps to fade before she headed for the closet. As she made her way down the hall, she could hear Tilly's wireless popping and crackling away, music floating out from under her door. Ava was sure that if life had turned out differently for Tilly, she would have ended up a music teacher or a concert pianist. Heidi's room followed, an aroma as sweet as her filling the air around her door. No doubt produced by the many bouquets of flowers she continually received from her customers. Heidi had been a florist before she arrived at the Zwinger, broke, widowed and in need of help. Zara, the Zwinger's Russian Doll and the most prickly of her girls, had the room next to Heidi's. There was a darker side to Zara that Ava had never been able to crack, the lock on her door, and her life, firmly in place. Maybe one day Zara would trust her enough to let her in.

Ava arrived at the closet which was next to Olga's room. She paused, thinking of the woman who was her first hire at the Zwinger. A lady of the night for many years, Olga had shown up in response to the somewhat cryptic advertisement Ava had put in the newspaper promoting the launch of her new business. She was loved for her busty bosom and liveliness, always keeping the men entertained with her quick wit.

And then there was Margot's room at the end of the hall. The Parisian Princess. Margot had been the second girl to show up at the Zwinger, looking for work. Ava had been surprised at her beauty, not just externally but internally as well. Margot had a light about her that was hard to come by in this line of work. She was genuine, strong and knew how to use her sexuality to her advantage. Ava deeply cherished their friendship, feeling as though Margot was more like a sister than a work colleague.

Ava paused at the closet door, her heart aching as she thought of all the girls who called the Zwinger home. She felt responsible for them, often wondering what would lie on the other side of the war for them all. Could life continue as it was? Or would the end of the war change them forever?

Ava pushed the thought aside as she slipped into the closet, quietly closing the door behind her. Unlocking the second compartment, she placed her finger to her lips, signalling the need to be quiet.

"I've made arrangements." She said quietly, stepping aside so the men could get out of the concealed compartment. "In 15 minutes I will take you out the back door where there will be a garbage truck waiting."

"Garbage?" A look of disgust crossed Eddie's face. Nathan whacked his shoulder in reprimand.

"Yes, a garbage truck." Ava replied. "The garbage truck will take you as far as the city line, before the trees, over on the west side of town. Do you know where I mean?"

"Yes." Nathan replied.

"Good. Once there he will knock three times on the back of the truck wall and wait only 5 minutes. You are to get out and make your own way from there. I'm sorry I couldn't get you any further away from the city."

"This is more than enough, thank you Ava." Nathan smiled.

"Now, you will need to change, you can't go outside in those uniforms, they will be looking for two soldiers." Ava turned, scanning the shelves in the closet and reaching for a basket. "This is our lost and found. I can't vouch for the quality of these clothes, but they are, at the very least, not a uniform." She handed the basket to Eddie who started to rifle through its contents, pulling out pants and crumpled shirts.

"There's only a single pair of pants and a couple of old shirts, do you have anything else?" Eddie looked up at Ava.

"Would a dress and some erotic underwear do?" She shot back.

"It's fine Eddie, we will make do." Nathan replied.

"Actually, I do." Ava's eyes looked Nathan up and down. "I'll be back in a moment." Ava slipped out of the closet and made her way to her bedroom. Kneeling beside the bed, her hands made fast work of locating the suitcase that laid hidden, the dust thick enough to carve a message into. She had promised herself she would eventually throw it away, but failed every time, the contents her only link to a life she no longer recognised. Ava ran her hand across the leather case, rubbing away the dust, revealing his name. *Jacob*. Her father. In this suitcase were the last of his possessions, mainly old clothes and the odd book. Ava clicked it open. It looked exactly as it did the day she had packed it.

"Papa," she whispered to the silence. "I hope you don't mind me giving your clothes away to some spies but I'm doing it to save our family." Ava let a heavy sigh fall from her lips, hoping it was true. She picked up the folded pants, shirts and jackets and quickly closed the suitcase, sliding it under her bed again, making her way back to the closet.

"Here." She said, as she handed the clothes to Nathan. "These should fit. Hurry up and change." Both men stood still. "What are you waiting for?" Ava demanded as Nathan and Eddie shot a glance between each other. Ava rolled her eyes. "Trust me boys, you have nothing I haven't already seen, but if it will make you comfortable, I'll turn around."

"Could I use the bathroom?" Eddie asked.

"Just get changed here, we're running out of time!" Ava protested.

"No, I really need to go. We've been in there a long while." Eddie pleaded.

"Fine. But be quick. It's the first door to the left." Eddie nodded and slipped out, leaving Nathan and Ava alone.

"Do you need the bathroom too?" She asked.

"Yes, but I'll go after." Nathan looked at Ava, waiting for her to turn around. She rolled her eyes again and faced the door, a flicker of disappointment crossing her chest. She wouldn't have minded seeing what was under that tough exterior.

"Ava?" Nathan asked, stripping down.

"Ja?"

She heard Nathan sigh deeply. Something wasn't right.

"What is it?" She pressed, dread beginning to creep in.

"I...I won't be able to get your family out of Dresden." He confessed.

Ava spun around, anger boiling up from within. "What!?" Ava moved towards him, cornering the pant-less man against the wall. "But you promised. You promised me!"

"Ava! Listen! Just listen. Please." Nathan pleaded, placing his hands on her shoulders, moving her away gently, as he turned her to face the door again. The sensation of his touch lingered on her skin and while she might had wanted to see his naked body, this was different.

"Listen carefully. What I'm about to tell you is highly classified and realistically, I could be discharged for giving top secret intel to a German. But you have been, well, exceptional in helping us, so I want to repay the favour." He paused, pulling on a shirt. "They're planning an air raid on Dresden. It's why we needed the location of the munitions factory and it's why I can't get you and your family out of Dresden just yet."

Ava's breath caught in her throat. "How much time do we have before they attack?"

"5 days. Maybe a week at most. It's just not enough time to get you out of here safely."

"I'll leave then. I'll get my family together and leave. Tonight, if I have to." Ava turned, panic rising within her. Nathan zipped up his pants, quickly tucking his shirt in.

"No, Ava, it's too dangerous." He shrugged on the jacket. Ava felt her heart twist in her chest. She wasn't prepared for how seeing her father's clothes on another man would make her feel. Especially a man who had the same coloured eyes as her father.

"Why?"

"Because an establishment like the Zwinger suddenly going dark will tip Richter off that something is about to go down." Ava looked away, Nathan's words matching what she already knew. Although, she had a hunch that the Zwinger going dark would not be what tipped Richter off. Rather it would be a missing piece of paper. "As crazy as it sounds," Nathan's voice drew Ava's attention. "staying here and pretending everything is normal is the safest thing you can do." He paused, scanning the room.

"Do you have a basement or somewhere safe you can go when the attack comes?"

"Ja. We have a basement." Ava nodded.

"Good. Start to gather supplies. Food. Blankets. Water. Whatever you need to last a week, at least, down there. Then, when the sirens sound, get your family together, and whoever else will fit into the basement, and hide. Do not, for *any* reason come out of the basement."

"But what if the building buries us in the air raid. We'll be trapped." Ava felt the panic rise within her.

"I will do everything I can to make sure they don't bomb this part of the city. I give you my word." Nathan was earnest in his promise, Ava knew that. If only it could have been a guarantee. "Now Ava, listen to me, this is the most important part. When you hear the bombing stop, wait three days. Do not, under any circumstances, come out of your basement, otherwise you might get caught in another wave."

"How will I know it's safe to come out?"

"I will come for you and your family." Nathan placed his hands on Ava's shoulders. "I will come for you." He repeated, wanting to cement his promise. Ava looked into his eyes and somehow knew he meant it. The proximity of his body causing those uncomfortable feelings to swirl within her again and she found herself wishing his hands would slide down her arms and around her waist and never let go. The thought unnerved her, but she couldn't pull herself away.

"How will I know it's you?" She asked, barely above a whisper. Nathan scanned the room searching for something. He looked down, a small smile forming at the corners of his mouth.

"Rosenfink." He said. Ava followed his gaze to the pin on her chest. "I'll call out for the Rosenfink." Ava's eyes met Nathan's again, her heart beginning to beat louder in her chest at the depth of meaning found in that sentence. Ava unpinned the little red bird from her lapel, sliding her hand up the jacket Nathan was wearing, she fastened it to the inside of the jacket.

"So you don't forget." She smiled.

"I could never forget you…" Nathan whispered in her hair. Ava glanced up and felt the heat of her own breath intertwine with his. She wasn't supposed to feel this way. She wasn't supposed to want it this much. But somewhere deep within her, desire called out. It was exhilarating and frightening all at the same time. Ava tilted her head slightly, willing Nathan to reach down and close the gap between them.

"Not like this…" He whispered. "Not like this…" Nathan stepped back, leaving Ava feeling exposed and rejected. Something she wasn't used to.

"What do you mean, 'Not like this?' You didn't seem to have a problem with it that night in the alley." Ava questioned, hurt lacing her voice. Nathan paused, his gaze unnerving Ava.

"I won't take what is not mine to have." He replied, gentleness in his tone.

"Wha-" The door clicked open, as Eddie slipped back into the room, halting any moment Ava and Nathan might have been having.

"All done." He whispered.

"Good. I'll be back." Nathan replied, not looking at Ava has he quickly made his way out the door. Ava's heart sank, which annoyed her. She had never allowed herself to get emotionally involved with any of her clients. It was messy and bad business practice. She swiftly pushed the incident aside and focussed back in on the task at hand, chiding herself for not just kissing him and getting it over and done with. It was just a kiss after all, it didn't mean anything. There were bigger things at stake and love, or whatever this feeling was, was not one of them. She looked up at Eddie.

"Clothes fit well." She commented, fixing his collar.

"Yeah they don't do too bad." Eddie straightened in a mock gentile stance. "Look like a regular aristocrat, I do." Ava let out a small laugh.

"Ava?" They both paused for second, eyes locked on the door. "Ava? It's Margot." Ava let out a sigh and opened the door, ushering her friend in.

"Did Joseph make it home safely?"

"Ja, ja. We managed to make it there without being followed. But there's a problem." Margot's face was solemn.

"What? Is it Joseph? My sister? My mother?" Panic began to fill Ava.

"Nein, they're all fine. But it would appear most of the German army is out hunting for these two. They were going door to door, asking people if they had seen two men and providing a description of you both. It's only a matter of time before they come back here and start tearing the place apart." Ava could see the fear in Margot's eyes. It matched her own.

"It's time to go then." Ava turned and opened the closet door, scanning the hallway. Nathan stepped out of the bathroom and met her gaze. She pressed her finger to her lips, reminding him to be quiet as she slipped out the door, Eddie and Margot close behind. The four of them made their way along the hall and down the back stairs to the kitchen. Thankfully, it was empty. Ava opened the back door and scanned the alleyway. It, too, was empty except for Otto's truck. She turned back.

"Margot, go tell Otto that the garbage will be ready to go in 2 minutes." Margot looked confused. "He'll understand, just go." Ava pleaded. Margot nodded and made her way into the saloon. "Follow me." Ava summoned the men. She moved quickly down that stairs, lifting up the flap on the garbage truck. Eddie climbed in first followed quickly by Nathan, who paused just before lowering the flap. He looked deep into Ava's eyes.

"Rosenfink." He whispered with a slight head nod, affirming again his promise to come for her. And with that he lowered the flap on the truck and disappeared from Ava's sight. She turned and made her way back inside, pausing just before closing the door. "Rosenfink." She whispered, part prayer, part promise, but mostly a plea. A plea for their safety and that every risk she had taken so far, would pay off.

4th February 9:48pm

The Zwinger was bustling with patrons, the patriotic energy powered by high spirits and the flowing liquor. Ava poured drinks and doted on her guests with a constant eye on the door. Richter was due, and she wasn't sure what kind of mood he was going to be in. The seconds ticked at a pace that did not match the pounding in her heart. No matter the amount of scolding she gave herself or alcohol she consumed, she couldn't slow the rise of panic in her chest.

Ava glanced at the clock. 9:50pm. Richter was usually here by now. But the doors to the saloon remained shut and his table occupied by some drunk soldiers.

"Have you seen him yet?" Margot whispered as she picked up a tray of drinks.

"Nein." Ava kept her eyes on the door.

"What does it mean if he doesn't come?"

Ava stared straight ahead. She had been pondering the same question for the last hour, with no conclusion.

"It could mean he has been sent into the field or…" Ava trailed off.

"Or what?" Margot pressed.

Ava sighed, keeping her eyes on the door, almost willing Richter to walk through so that she knew what she was about to say wasn't true.

"Or what Ava?" Margot urged.

"Or he found the garbage we threw out."

TEN

The Hair Dye

5th February 9:24am

Ava dressed herself quickly and downed the last of her coffee. After a fretful night's sleep, she was already on her second cup and felt a third would not be far behind. Her mind was in a constant state of ebb and flow, like a ship rolling through rough sea. She couldn't still it. Couldn't quiet it. And no matter what she drank, she couldn't silence it. Fear and worry constantly swirled in her stomach, adding to the sense that everything was unravelling, fast.

Richter had not shown last night, and she didn't know why.

Pushing the barrage of questions that consumed her aside, she put her hat on, taking in the full view of her outfit. Her favourite navy dress hugged her curves in all the right places. The polka dot detail added a touch of sweetness to the dress. Normally, this outfit would make her feel beautiful, empowered and strong. Today, it did nothing to lift her spirits.

Ava grabbed her bag, checking she had all she needed and made her way downstairs. The saloon sat in silence with the rest of the house, no one awake yet to ask where she was going or what she was doing. The hustle of the street greeted her along with the smells of a town starting its day. Ava paused for a moment, watching the people of Dresden go about their business, none the wiser to the impending doom. The atmosphere was filled with the dread of war and it hung around the city like an inescapable smell of decay. This town, that had once been so alive, now seemed like an old dog, weary and waiting to die. Or be put out of its misery.

If Nathan had made it out of the city last night then he would be on his way to reporting the location of the secret munitions factory to Allied forces. Which meant they had 5 days, a week at most, before a bullet would be put through the head of the decaying-dog city of Dresden. The very thought broke Ava's heart. What had she done?

She stepped out onto the footpath and began to make her way towards the flat. Every choice she had made up until that point had been driven by the desire to save her family. It was only now that she realised her well-intentioned decisions meant death and destruction for many others. She swallowed the nauseated feeling that rose within her. All she could do was hope that in some way, somehow, the destruction of the munitions factory would have little to no human casualties. At least that's what Nathan had told her. A man who had promised to get her and her family out of Dresden but couldn't make that happen before the bombing. A man with a fake name and an allegiance to Germany's enemy. A man who had not left her mind, since he had left her house. All Ava could do was pray that the spy was telling the truth.

Pray. Was that really all she could do? She had barely uttered two-words to Yahweh since she was fourteen and now she was praying? He hadn't heard her before and there would be no reason he would start now. And yet, the tug on her heart to pray was consistent. Ava ignored it. Her prayers were useless, God did not listen to people who kill other people.

"Why do you bother with us, Yahweh?" She mumbled to the wind. "Why would you bother with me?" A question she was sure, as always, would go unanswered.

Everything seemed unstable now. Richter, the spies, her family, the Zwinger. Her entire life could be blown away in a single moment, rendering all her worry and fear completely pointless.

A heavy sigh released from her as she stood at the doorway of the apartment, feeling the weight of the responsibility, not just for the safety of her family, but all of Dresden too. Why had she been given such a mantle? What could Yahweh want with a brothel madame in the middle of Nazi Germany? By His standards she was a sinner, living in one of the most sinful countries in the world. And yet, for reasons she would never understand, He had used her to gather the information that could bring an early end the war and potentially save her family.

Brushing aside questions she would never be able to answer, Ava squared her shoulders back, preparing herself for the conversation she was about to have with her family.

⁓

"You what!?" Hila's eyes flared with shock and anger. "Hadar, are you out of your mind?" She demanded.

"Mama, List-"

"Boys. Go to your room. Your Oma and Mama need to speak to your Tanté. Alone." Hila commanded.

"No, Mama. They need to hear this too." Ava held her ground. "Plus, Joseph already knows. The errand I sent him on yesterday was to deliver the information to the spies."

"WHAT!?" Hila's anger bubbled over. "You sent your own nephew to aid Allied spies? After all your talk of keeping us safe, you send him to do something that would surely mean the end of his life, and ours, if found out?"

"Mama, keep you voice down!" Ava demanded. "Yes, I sent Joseph into danger, but, thankfully, he wasn't hurt or caught. However, the Nazi's are looking for a boy who meets his description." Ava watched Hila and Ayala's eyes grow wide. "Jose-"

"I accidentally ran into a Nazi soldier and he started yelling at me. Nathan, one of the spies, tried to help but he accidentally did this," Joseph held up his hand. "and that set them off. We ran all the way to Tanté's place where she hid us and got rid of the soldiers who had followed us. Then Margot, Tanté's friend, brought me home to make sure I got back safely. Tanté asked me to not tell you what had happened but rather say I had gotten lost. But it's ok Mama and Oma because I am safe. We didn't get caught." Ava's heart warmed at Joseph's attempt to defend her. Ayala sank into the seat behind her, the shock of the truth too much.

"I know this is a lot to take in and I understand your anger, but you all need to come with me, right now." Ava pleaded.

"Where?" Hila demanded.

"To the Zwinger."

"What?" Hila's eyes raged.

"Mama, please. I know you're all angry and I understand, but I don't think it's safe for you to stay here anymore."

"Because of your actions." Hila let the comment hit its mark. And it did. Ava bit back the tears.

"Yes." Ava swallowed, the tension hanging thick in the room. "Please. I need you to trust me on this." Ava knelt down to meet her sister's eyes, hoping to win her support. "Please, Ayala. I know you feel as though I was dishonest, but everything I told you yesterday was true. It's just things have changed now and it's no longer safe for you to be here. Please, trust me on this." She repeated.

"Trust you?" Ayala's eyes grew wide with rage. "Trust you? You put my son directly in danger yesterday and now the Nazis are looking for him. Let alone the fact you let him into that pit of sin you call a home! A place I told you my children were never to know about!" Ayala stood. "And you want me to trust you?" The tears that formed at the corners of Ayala's eyes broke Ava's heart.

"I'm so sorry sister." Ava looked down. "I'm sorry for the pain I have caused you. For not telling you the whole truth and for putting Joseph in danger. But I need you to understand, I did it so that I could keep you safe. The information Joseph delivered to the spies could end the war-"

"Get out." Ayala's face was a steely cold. Ava had never seen her sister so angry and it unnerved her.

"Ayala, please-"

"Get. Out." Ayala said again, sterner then last. Ava went to plead her case again. "I mean it Ava." Ayala cut her off before she could get a word out. "Take your fake name and your fake care for this family and get out. I never want to see your face again!"

Ava looked at her mother, silently pleading for her understanding but it was clear where her allegiances laid. Ava stood and squared her shoulders back, reaching into her bag.

"Fine. I'll leave. But please think about what I said. You would be safe with me at the Zwinger." Ava placed the box of hair dye on the table. "I brought you this. It's probably a good idea to dye Joseph's hair." Tension hung in the air like a thick fog, amplified by the silence of her family. "I'll show myself out." Ava said barely above a whisper and made her way to the door.

10th February 8:28pm

To: Agent Sinclair.

From: Secretary of State for Air, Sir Sinclair.

Subject: URGENT UPDATE - Operation Thunderclap

Excellent work son. Frankland very impressed with intel. Operation Thunderclap is moving ahead. Weather permitting, Pathfinders will be dropped on February 13th, followed by Plate Rack soon after with blockbusters. Focus on communication towers, railways and secret munitions factory. This will shorten the war and hinder German war efforts thanks to you.

Report to Allied HQ and debrief. We have another assignment for you and Flannagen.

Nathan scrunched the decoded telegram in his hand.

"Bad news?" Eddie asked, as he puffed on his cigarette.

"Not exactly. They received the intel. They'll bomb in three days." Nathan began to walk down the street. They had arrived in Görlitz two days ago, having taken their time making their way to the now Allied occupied city. What would have been a two-day hike turned into a four-day crawl as they blindly made their way through thick bush and off-the-beaten-track roads in order to avoid capture. Eddie had returned after a food scout one afternoon with a local newspaper brandishing an artist's impression of their faces. Richter must have sent word to the surrounding towns, warning of the Allied spies on the run and though the artists impression looked nothing like them, they still opted to keep a low profile.

As soon as they had arrived in Görlitz, they had immediately tracked down Allied soldiers and were able to get the intel to High Command that night. Nathan stared out across the street. He had done his job well and yet felt, for the first time, a sense of guilt over it. The bombing was coming and there was no way of getting word to Ava.

"Well that's good." Eddie chirped, his comment cutting across Nathan's occupied mind.

"Is it?" Nathan asked, more to himself than to Eddie.

"Of course it is." Eddie responded. "We got them what they wanted and now those bloody German Nazis will get what's coming to them."

"And what about the German civilians?" Nathan asked defensively.

"Civilians or one particular civilian?" Eddie shot back. Nathan looked ahead, not answering Eddie's questioning gaze.

"Look old chap," Eddie pulled on Nathan's arm, stopping both of them. "You've done all you can. You told her to get herself and her family to the basement and you provided the coordinates of the Zwinger so the bombers can avoid it. You can't do anything more than what you have. So let's go get some food, have a few pints and tomorrow we'll head back to London to receive our next mission.

There'll always be more women, Nath." Eddie reasoned as he continued walking.

Nathan knew he was right. They should just head back to London and get on with it. The war wasn't over yet and he'd sworn allegiance to his country. That meant being of service to them indefinitely. What he hadn't anticipated, was the way Ava had infiltrated his thoughts since he'd climbed into the back of the garbage truck. The entire trip he had been praying for her, pleading with God to keep her safe. He had never felt this way about any woman before, the moment in the closet playing on repeat. The proximity of her body while he was practically naked had nearly undone him. He had wanted her, there was no denying it. But he had wanted her to want him back, not just give him what she thought he wanted. He wanted her heart, more than he wanted her body, and that seemed firmly locked away.

It wasn't just her beauty that drew him in, it was her strength, her conviction, her incredibly sharp mind. Smuggling them out via a garbage truck was brilliant. She was clearly smart and creative. The lucrative business she had been able to carve out for herself was impressive, given the times. And while it wasn't the most pure of endeavours, she had clearly made the most out of the situation. But it was the love for her family he admired most. And it was the very thing that made him feel racked with guilt. She was risking everything to get her family out of Germany and he'd promised to help her do that. But it was a promise he wasn't sure he could keep.

"Come on Sinclair! Let's go find us some food." Eddie called out, drawing Nathan's attention back to the present.

"Coming." Nathan muttered to himself. His body might be in Görlitz, but his mind, and heart, were firmly planted in a brothel in Dresden.

ELEVEN

The Cigar

12th February, 9:15pm

Ava's breath caught in her chest as Richter stamped slush from his boots, the door shutting behind him. It had been over a week since he had last visited the Zwinger. He looked up and immediately met Ava's gaze, his steely cold eyes communicating a quiet fury Ava had never seen before. Her hope of his absence being a sign that he had been deployed to the field, diminished. If he was this angry, then something was wrong. Something was very wrong. Fear gripped her body rendering her motionless as he made his way towards the bar, not letting her gaze go. Ava tried to swallow the lump in her throat, but her mouth had dried up.

"Gut - uh ah - Guten Abend Lieutenant General. Drink?" Ava managed get out around the desert in her mouth. She held her stature as high as she could, trying to hide the sick feeling of fear growing in her stomach.

"Ja."

Ava lifted the glass onto the counter and poured him his regular shot of schnapps. Richter threw it back and slammed the glass on the counter, drawing the attention of the patrons around him.

"More?" Ava asked. He nodded in response and so she poured him another. He repeated the process, slamming the shot glass down.

"Is there something the matter Lieutenant General?" Ava asked, lacing her tone with as much sweetness as she could muster.

"9:45." He replied, turning on his heel and storming over to his regular table.

"You ok?" Margot asked, appearing beside Ava.

"I'm fine. I think. He's upset about something." Ava whispered to Margot as she poured the beers. "Take these to his table and tell him they're on the house."

"You don't think…" Margot's voice trailed off, leaving the question that was on both their minds hanging in the air.

"I'll find out at 9:45."

Ava drew in one more breath, hoping it would deliver a surge of courage to her rattled bones. It steadied her nerves for a fleeting second, but they came rushing back. It was showtime, regardless of the swarm of butterflies that had taken up residence in her stomach. As she stepped out the back door, she pulled her shawl tighter, clutching at what little security she could find there. Richter was waiting for her, puffing away on a cigar, staring up at the stars. Ava stopped beside him, a tension filling the space between them. They stood in silence for a few moments, which only served to heighten Ava's growing fear. She just wanted to get this over with.

"Tilly reported this morning that the Führer's visit has been post-poned. She didn't have any more infor-"

In one swift move, Richter had grabbed Ava by the throat and slammed her up against the wall, pinning her with his body, knocking the air out of her momentarily. She scrambled to breathe again, clawing at his hand, eyes wide with the fear that coursed through her veins. He only needed to squeeze a little tighter or hold his grip a little longer.

"Shut up whore!" Richter spat at her. "I do not care for your lies." He released his grip enough to let her breathe again but didn't remove his hand from her throat. Ava sucked in the air as quickly and as deeply as her lungs could handle.

"Tonight, I will do the talking." He sucked on his cigar, breathing the foul fumes on her face. Ava coughed at the sticky, dry smoke filling her already parched throat.

"Now, my little Kolibri. Let's start with telling me the truth about the spies."

"What do you mean? I told you everything I know." Ava coughed.

Richter slapped her, wrapping his hand around her throat again. "Do not lie to me whore! They have not been back since you told me about them. So you must have given them what they wanted!" He bellowed.

"And how would I do that? I don't know where the munitions factory is." She yelled back. Richter slapped her again.

"Do not be so disrespectful, you filthy Jewish parasite! If you are so innocent, then why is there a page missing from my book? The same page that contained the location of a secret underground munitions factory in Dresden? A page that just happened to go missing the night I was in your room!" Rage seethed in his eyes.

Ava's mind raced as she fought to steady her pulse. She needed to regain control of the situation.

"If it is missing, it's not my doing." Ava swallowed, steadying herself. "One of the other girls must have taken it from your pocket. I was with you the whole time. But if you let me go, I will find out if there is a fox in my hen house." Ava replied, keeping a measured tone to her voice.

"Wrong again!" Richter yelled, pressing the lit end of his cigar against Ava's bare arm. She screamed in pain. "When will you learn, my little kolibri, that I always get what I want?" He leaned in and licked her ear. Ava tried to silence the whimper that escaped her lips but her arm was throbbing from the searing pain.

"I told you, I don't know anything." Ava said through gritted teeth, trying to keep the tears that burned at the back of her eyes at bay.

"Stop lying to me, Ava. I don't like it when you keep secrets!" He lifted his hand to strike her again.

"OK!" Ava yelled, the sound pausing Richter's hand. "Ok, I'll tell you." Richter's countenance changed slightly. "I'm listening."

"Yes. The spies were here." Richter's hand loosened. Ava forced down a dry swallow, wishing she had something to ease the fire in her throat and on her arm. "They came back the following night. I told them that I couldn't help them find the munitions factory but if they wanted it, then the little black book in your pocket would be the best place to start. Maybe they somehow broke into your house and stole the piece of paper." Ava took a breath, hoping he would buy the lie. She needed to redirect his focus.

"Ok." Richter suddenly stepped back, releasing his grip on Ava. She fell to the ground, immediately grabbing snow to place on her burned flesh. The relief was instant but short lived. Richter stood, his back to Ava, smoking his cigar. Ava heaved in breath after breath and rubbed her throat, the feeling of Richter's hand burned into her skin.

"Are we done?" She whispered, desperately wanting to escape.

"Done?" Richter turned with a look in his eyes that made Ava's skin go cold. Richter stormed back over to her and hurled her back against the wall, holding her there with his arm across her chest, pressing into her throat again. "We are done when I say we're done." He said through gritted teeth, moving his hand down her thigh and lifting her skirt. He ran his hand under her underwear, a hungry look in his eye. Ava tried to not respond, to go to the place she went when a man was taking what he wanted from her, but fear kept her present and alert, acutely aware of Richter's hands. It was at that moment Ava realised that if Richter wanted her dead or sent to a concentration camp, he would have done it already. He still wanted something more from her and maybe it was just her body, but she could try and use that to her advantage. She felt a surge within her to fight.

"Is this how you want to do this?" She asked. "Our first time together, here in a dirty alley?" She scanned his eyes.

"It seems suitable. A dirty alley for a dirty whore." Richter breathed heavily, licking and kissing her neck while undoing his belt with his free hand, keeping her pinned to the wall with his body. His cigar, wedged between his fingers, dancing dangerously close to Ava's face.

"Wouldn't we be more comfortable in my room?" Ava suggested, trying to keep her voice measured while her mind ran crazy searching for an escape route.

"Well, you see, my little Kolibri, I find that when I go to your bedroom, things go missing." He let the sentence land, waiting for her to react. Ava kept her face blank. She needed to keep her composure if she was going to get out of this.

"Come to think of it, kolibri, there is one more thing I want from you before I take you. Tell me, who lives in the apartment you visited last week?"

Ava felt the colour drain from her face, silently hoping the dark night would hide it from Richter. "What apartment?" She managed to get out.

"The one you visit every day, according to your neighbours. Apparently, two children live there?" He puffed on his cigar, keeping his arm across her chest. Ava needed to think quickly.

"It's an elderly woman who I sit with some days to provide company. She is all by herself. As for the two boys, I have no idea who they are. I just see them playing in the street some days." Ava watched as Richter's eyes narrowed, a sinister look in them.

"Lieutenant General! Lieutenant General!" Hans yelled out into the night air. Richter stepped back, letting Ava once again fall to the ground. He put his cigar in his mouth, zipping up his pants.

"Ja!? What is it?" He yelled back, stepping into the light. Hans turned and began to make his way over to him, doing a double take when he saw Ava hunched over on the ground, holding snow against her arm.

"We've received an urgent telegram requesting you to return to base immediately." Hans explained.

"Fine. Get the car ready. I will meet you out front." Hans clicked his heels together "Hail Hitler!" He threw his hand in the air and then turned with military precision on his heel, making his way back inside. Richter turned and knelt down, tilting Ava's chin to meet his eyes.

"Do not look so relieved little kolibri. We are not done here. I will be back."

"I told you everything I know." Ava tried to look convincing, but the sinister chuckle left Richter's lips left her feeling defeated. "No, little kolibri, I don't think you did." He released a puff of cigar smoke in her face. "You see, I never said it was two boys who lived there." He smiled, like a cat who had just caught the bird. He stood up. "We'll chat again soon, kolibri." Ava watched from her peripherals as he disappeared around the corner.

The tears came thick and fast, pouring forth from the depths of Ava's heart. The exhaustion from all she had been carrying the last few weeks finally broke her. She had done everything she could to keep her family safe and now Richter knew about them, or at least that someone of significance lived in that building. It would only be a matter of time before he figured out who they were and then it would be all over. She would lose them all, forever. Ava heaved, trying to stifle her tears. The pain in her arm throbbed but it was nothing compared to the pain in her heart. Had she sentenced them all to death? Regret began to fill her. If only she had not agreed to help Nathan, none of this would be happening. But then she would also not know of the impending air raid and they would all be lost anyway. She clumsily wiped the tears from her cheeks and sat back on her knees, the cold beginning to make itself known. Ava felt numbness take over her body and mind. She was losing her will to fight. Her family were angry with her. There was no way of knowing if Nathan would return. And now Richter knew about the most important thing in her life. What was the point, she may as well give herself over to Richter and be done with it. Death looked far more attractive than living did anyway.

Ava tried to calm the tears, releasing a hopeless sigh. Just then, something caught her attention, beyond the glow of the light that spilled out of the Zwinger and into the alleyway. She paused, trying to make out what the tiny figure was. A little rose finch hopped into the pool of light. Ava stared at the little bird as it flittered about, pecking at the snow. In that moment, the world seemed to cease turning as she watched the little bird that had come to symbolise so much to her.

"Papa....is that you?" Ava whispered to the bird. The finch continued to hop around, completely at ease in Ava's presence. "Papa...I'- I'm so sorry. I tried...I tried so hard to protect them... but I failed. I failed you." Ava slumped into the snow, completely defeated.

The bird hopped over towards Ava, flittering into her lap. She froze. Never once, for all her trying, had a Rosenfink come to her, let alone willingly land in her lap. She remained completely still wondering how such a small creature could feel so at ease in the face of such uncertainty. The bird wouldn't have known if Ava was a friend or foe, and yet, here it was, resting in her lap.

Deep in her spirit Ava felt a strange reassurance swell within. She released a slow breath. Maybe if this tiny bird could show trust and faith in the face of danger, she could too. The war was not over yet. There was still time to fight.

The little finch jumped off her lap. Ava watched it hop around for a moment longer. Wearily, she pulled herself to her feet. Suddenly, everything felt clear and she knew what she needed to do. A fresh surge of courage filled Ava as she looked down at the bird. In the blink of an eye it was gone. Off into the darkness, unafraid.

Ava pulled her shawl around her and looked up at the sky, feeling again the strange sensation that something or someone was present. Maybe it was her Papa. Maybe it was Yahweh. Either way, she didn't judge the feeling, allowing herself, for the first time in a long time, to let the peace of his presence surface within her.

"Ava?" Margot called out from the back step. "Ava?"

"I'm here." She called back, stepping into the light.

"Ava, your arm and face! What happened? Are you ok?" Margot hurried to Ava's side.

"I'm fine. Can you look after things here?" Ava asked.

"Of course, but where are you going?"

"To get my family. " Ava replied.

"Are you sure it's safe enough to bring them here, now, with the place so full?"

Ava looked into Margot's eyes, feeling completely certain of her decision. "It's now or never."

The sound of the front door opening woke Hila from her slumber immediately, adrenalin quickly replacing deep sleep. She rolled over to see Ayala sitting up in bed.

"What was that?" She croaked, rubbing the sleep from her eyes.

"I don't know but stay here Mama." Ayala threw the covers back, grabbed her robe and made her way out of the bedroom. Hila wasn't one to sit still, so while she was a little slower than her youngest daughter, she was not going to stay put. Her old bones creaked as she put her robe on and followed Ayala out. She was surprised to see her eldest daughter standing in the doorway having a heated whispered conversation with her sister.

"Hadar, what is wrong?" Ava stepped around her sister, making her way towards Hila.

"Mama, we need to leave. Now." Ava's eyes shone with an urgency Hila had never seen before. Her eldest daughter was always so composed, so together, so strong. What Hila saw in Hadar's eyes tonight was something different.

"Why, Hadar, what has happened?" Hila demanded.

"I can't explain it all right now, but they know about you."

"Who knows about us?" Ayala demanded.

"The Nazis. I need to get you to safety. The only place I can keep you safe is with me, at the Zwinger."

"Absolutely not!" Ayala protested. "There is no way we're stepping foot in that place."

"Please Ayala, I know you are angry with me right now and I understand why but I wouldn't be here if I didn't think your lives were in danger. Please, please, come with me, now." She pleaded again. Hila had never seen Hadar like this which made her wonder if her eldest daughter might have good reason to be panicked. Just then, the door to the boy's room opened as a bleary-eyed Joseph emerged wanting to know what was happening. The light it threw onto Hadar's face revealed bruising around her eye and cheek and the white bandage, clumsily around her arm, glowed like a beacon.

"Hadar, your face!" Hila raised her hand, lightly touching the bruising that had formed. "What happened? Who did this?"

"I'll explain everything, I promise. Right now, we *need* to leave." Hila stared deep into her daughter's eyes and for the first time could see the fear and the courage all at once.

"Joseph, go back to bed, your Tanté was just leaving." Ayala said sternly to her eldest.

"No." Hila looked over at Joseph. "We're going with your Tanté. Joseph, go pack some clothes for both you and Levi. We will leave in 5 minutes."

"Mama!" Ayala protested.

"Ayala, we are going." Hila shut down the conversation. "Now, go and pack some things for both of us. Leave everything else. We only need our clothes." She commanded. Ayala begrudgingly went to their room to pack. Hila turned back to Hadar.

"Danke, Mama." She said softly. "I'm sorry, I'm so sorry." Tears rolled down her cheeks as her mother reached up, wrapping her arms around her daughter.

"It's ok, mein Liebchen, it's ok. Yahweh will protect us." Hila whispered into Hadar's hair, hoping she was right.

TWELVE

The Sound of Sirens

1 **3th February, 9:23am**

Ava smiled at her youngest nephew, chewing away on his breakfast, dropping crust and crumbs everywhere, blissfully unaware of where he was or the danger he was in. Oh, to be so innocent.

"Levi, don't make a mess." Ayala unnecessarily scolded her youngest.

"He's fine, Ayala. I'll clean it up later." Ava said, smiling at the boy.

"Well we wouldn't want to mess up such a fine establishment." She replied, her tone dripping with disgust and sarcasm. Ava stifled the desire to erupt at her younger sister who had been ungrateful and disrespectful since arriving at the Zwinger late last night. Ava had managed to smuggle them through the back door and straight down into the basement, shielding them from seeing anything that would make them uncomfortable. She had then made sure they had blankets, food and light. She had seen to their every need for their own protection and still Ayala begrudged her sister.

"Ayala." Hila reprimanded. "Stop being so ungrateful." She scolded, keeping her eyes on her knitting.

"Tanté?" Joseph piped up, diverting the conversation. "How long do we need to be down here?"

A sympathetic smile formed on Ava's face. "I wish I knew, Joseph." She stifled a yawn. "For now, though, you need to stay down here and you need to be quiet. No one can know you are here."

"What about Margot?" Joseph asked. "Can she visit with us?"

"Maybe." Ava looked at her watch. "I have some errands to run. We're going to need more food and a few other supplies if you're going to be here for a while." She ruffled his hair.

"How long are you going to keep us here?" Ayala's eyes flared with anger.

"As long as necessary." Ava replied, more sternly than she should have, fatigue beginning to get the better of her.

"You're just going to keep us locked down here? Living like rats in your filthy basement? You haven't even told us why we're here or what has put us in such danger, let alone why you have bruises on your face!" Ava knew her sister didn't approve of her lifestyle, but she had never truly understood the depths of her disgust until now. Ava was beginning to see that no amount of explaining would ever change that. A small pang of jealousy circled Ava's heart as she wondered what it must be like to have lived such a virtuous life. A life that wasn't burdened by atonement. Would it ever be enough to make up for what she had done?

Ignoring her sister's demand, Ava stood, the weight of their situation pressing in on her. Glancing out the basement window to the alleyway, the finch from the night before appeared in her mind, along with the strange sense of peace she had felt. She didn't know how, but she was going to get them out of this, alive.

"I need to get those supplies." Ava replied, disregarding the frustrated expression on her sister's face. "Stay down here, do not, under any circumstances, leave this room."

"That won't be hard, you've kept us locked away from the world all this time, why should now be any different." Ayala spat back.

"Trust me Ayala, it's not a world you want to be apart of." Ava turned and walked up the stairs, firmly locking the door behind her.

13th February, 8:44pm

The Zwinger Bordell was in full swing as normal, the beer flowing, the women half dressed, the men salivating at their exposed flesh. With the atmosphere of merriment, it was hard to believe there was a war going on at all. Only Ava felt the impending doom of the evening as she watched the door, waiting for Richter to arrive. With Margot's help she had managed to cover up the bruising the had formed on her cheek and right eye. A long sleeved top took care of the dressing covering the cigar burn. She ached all over, not just from Richter throwing her around the night before but from the heaviness of it all. It felt like her insides were a contortionist putting on the greatest performance of their life. She couldn't seem to settle herself long enough to eat or drink. Her mind kept dragging her back to her family, hidden beneath the floorboards and an angry Richter set to burst through those doors any moment.

How had the delicate balance of her life shifted so quickly? It had been, what, two weeks since the spies had walked into the Zwinger? And somehow, during that wisp of time, everything had changed. The noose of blackmail Richter held over her head was dangling precariously close to her neck and Ava would willingly step into it, if it meant her family would be safe.

The smashing of glass brought her attention back into the room. She had dropped a glass. Third one of the night. Herman began to make his way towards her.

"It's fine Herman. Keep serving, I'll clean it up." Ava knelt down to pick up the glass, Margot appearing at her side.

"Margot, I'm fine. You don't need to help with this." Ava said a little too sternly.

"Are you ok?" She asked ignoring, Ava's comment.

"I'm fine. Just a little distracted."

"Ja. It's obvious."

"Sorry." Ava looked down.

Margot's face softened. "We're going to get through this." Ava could see in Margot's eyes her earnestness and for a split second, Ava felt the tinniest bit lighter.

"Are they settled?" Ava asked, continuing to wipe up the liquid.

"Yes, the boys are blissfully unaware and your sister is still as steely silent as always. Your Mama however is going to make me a scarf." Margot smiled. Ava wasn't sure how she would have made it through half of what they had these past few weeks if it weren't for Margot.

"Thank you, Margot, for everything." Ava smiled back.

"You're welcome." Margot replied. "You would have done the same for me. Now, quit it with all the mushy stuff. You're dampening the mood!" She winked. Just then, there was a noticeable shift in the atmosphere. The room quietened and tension seemed to take the place of the light heartedness that was present only seconds earlier. Ava and Margot looked at each other, slowly rising to their feet.

Like clockwork, the door had swung open at 9:35pm, Richter standing within its frame. There was a darkness to him tonight, Ava noticed, as he walked towards the bar. A darkness Ava had never seen before. Ava squared her shoulders back and lifted herself to her full height. If he had come to fight then she was going to give him one hell of a battle.

"Guten Abend Lieutenant General, can I get you a drink?" She asked.

Richter didn't respond as Klaus and Hans made their way around the bar, gripping Ava's arms.

"Outside. Now."

Ava tilted her chin towards Richter, looking him square in the eye. "Tell them to get their hands off me first." She held his gaze for a few seconds before he nodded, and his goons released their grip.

"Margot, look after the place. I'll be back soon." She said pointedly at Richter who led the way into the alley. Klaus and Hans fell in step behind her. As they passed the basement, Ava breathed in all the courage she could muster. Tonight, Richter could do whatever he wanted to her, she no longer cared. He couldn't touch her family and that was all that mattered.

Once outside, Richter stood with his back to Ava, Hans and Klaus behind her, a few steps away.

"Are they really necessary?" Ava asked.

Richter didn't respond. He just kept staring up at the night sky.

"Are they really necessary?" Ava repeated the question, more annoyed.

"The sky is quite clear tonight, isn't it kolibri?" Richter ignored her question. "It is crystal clear, considering it has been cloudy most of the day." Richter paused again, still not turning to face Ava. "Isn't that the interesting thing about clouds. In one moment, they can hide the sun, keep it from us and then the next, be gone, making things clear again." He turned to face her. "Much like you." Ava didn't like the look in his eyes. He moved closer to her and she instinctively took a step back, bumping into Hans and Klaus. She was surrounded.

"I don't know what you mean." Ava replied, feeling as though courage was rising within her from a deep well she had never known was there.

"Oh, come now kolibri. Did you really think I wouldn't find out? Did you really think you could outsmart me? You Jews are so stupid." He shook his head mockingly, waiting for her to catch on. Ava remained still. Richter rolled his eyes and reached into his jacket pocket, pulling a small folded piece of paper and handing it to Ava. Confused, she opened it, her heart dropping as she realised it was the missing piece of paper from Richter's book.

"This, kolibri. This." He said, a hint of anger lacing his voice. "Look familiar? I'm sure it does, considering you ripped it from my book." His countenance darkened. "I don't like it when things are hidden from me. I especially don't like it when my pets steal from me!" He moved towards her. "Where are the spies, Ava?" The anger was growing in Richter's voice.

"I don't know." Her response was met with a hard slap across her face.

"Wrong answer!" Richter replied. "Where are the spies?" He demanded again.

"I don't know." Ava responded and again Richter slapped her. She resolved to not cower or whimper. She wasn't going to give him the satisfaction.

"Fine. If you won't tell me what I want, maybe your mother or sister will tell me what I need to know. Or maybe your beloved nephews?" Richter's evil smile spread across his face as Ava felt the world give way from beneath her feet. "You thought I didn't know." He said, clearly satisfied with her reaction. "I know everything, Kolibri."

Ava's breathing quickened, panic rising inside of her. How had he found them? Did someone see her the night before? Did one of the girls tell him? Ava realised the million questions that flooded her mind were pointless. All she could do now was somehow bargain with Richter for their safety. He had found her weakness…but she knew his.

"Well done, Richter." Ava commented, watching the smug look on his face shift slightly. "You found out about my family. Well done. It's only taken you two years. And to think the entire time they were right under your nose." Ava let out a mocking laugh. "You may have found my weakness Richter, but I have known yours all along." Tension grew between them but she didn't stop. She didn't care anymore. She was done being trapped in his cage of blackmail. "It didn't take much. I didn't have to come up with some elaborate plan. I didn't have to spend hours or days figuring out how to get the information from you. All I had to do was offer you something you could never have. Me." Richter landed another slap but this only spurred Ava on.

"That night in my room, everything I said about the spies was true. Not a single word of it was a lie. I just failed to mention that I had agreed to help them. And I did that right under your nose." Richter hit her again, this time the subtle taste of blood coloured Ava's tongue. She had hit a nerve, and she wasn't about to stop.

"Your obsession with power makes you vulnerable, Richter."

"And your love for your family makes you weak." He spat back at her. "Make no mistake, Ava, we will get them and torture them within an inch of their lives right in front of you. And you will be powerless to stop it. Now, tell me where the spies are!"

Ava went to say something but stopped, paused by Richter's last sentence.

"You don't know where they are, do you?" Ava said slowly, realising that Richter was more exposed than she first thought. A smile formed on her lips. "First the spies evade you and now my family....Oh Richter. That must just grind you, doesn't it? You strut around here as though you own this town when in reality, you're just as weak as the Nazi war effort. You have no-"

Richter hit Ava again, harder this time. "Shut up, whore!" He yelled. Ava spat the blood in her mouth onto the snow covered ground. Richter grabbed her hair and pulled her head back. "I will find your family and I *will* kill them." Richter seethed, his eyes wild with rage.

"No, you won't. Because you can't see past your own nose." She laughed at him and he shoved her head forward, turning his back. "I was hiding the spies in the closet upstairs, you fool!" Ava continued, pressing in on his shattered pride. "And you believed me when I told you they had run towards the field!" Ava laughed again. A laugh that tipped Richter over and was answered with another slap.

"Hold her!" Richter commanded Hans and Klaus as he rolled up his sleeves. Ava knew she was about to be beaten within an inch of her life but she didn't care. Richter could take whatever he wanted, but he would never have her family.

"I'll never tell you where they are." Ava seethed at him. "I'll never tell you anything again."

"We'll see about that." Richter came for her, but as he was about to land the first punch, the sound of air raid sirens rung out across the crystal clear night, screaming of impending destruction. Richter looked off in their direction, then back at Ava.

"That sounds like an Allied air raid. I wonder where they'll bomb first?" Ava mocked, blood staining her teeth. Furious, Richter landed a punch in Ava's gut, knocking the breath out of her as she fell to her knees. He gripped her hair, pulling her head back.

"We're not done." He replied, releasing her head. "Come." Richter marched off towards the car, Klaus and Hans close behind.

"Good luck...getting out...alive." Ava whispered to the sound of sirens.

THIRTEEN

The Chaos

3th February, 9:51pm

Pulling herself up off the ground, Ava's breath slowly returned as she stumbled her way inside. The sirens had plunged the Zwinger into pandemonium as patrons scrambled to get to safety. The sound of the first bombs being dropped in the distance amplified the panic. Ava knew she needed to get down to the basement but she wasn't about to abandoned her girls.

"Is there a shelter!? Do we have a shelter!?" Heidi screamed at Ava, gripping her shoulders. Ava placed her hand on Heidi's arms, hoping to calm the fear in her eyes.

"Yes, Heidi, we do, but we need to get the other girls. Go check the rooms upstairs and meet me back here. Ok?" Heidi nodded and took off upstairs. Ava made her way into the saloon, immediately locating Margot.

"Ava, your face!" Margot exclaimed.

"Get to the basement. Now!" Ava yelled at her. Margot did as she was told. The bombing seemed to be getting louder, as Ava frantically checked the back rooms and bathrooms.

Hurrying back to the kitchen, she found Margot waiting with Heidi, Olga and Tilly.

"Where's Zara?" She asked, panicked.

"She left, with one of the patrons. Herman ran off too." Tilly replied. Ava shook her head. There was no time to find them now. She pulled the key to the basement out of her pocket and frantically opened the door. "Quickly." She said, stepping aside to let the girls go first. Ava did one more scan of the room and offered up a prayer for Zara. There was nothing more she could do. She closed the basement door behind her, locking it from the inside and made her way down the stairs, the sound of the bombing getting slightly more faint, but no less fear-inducing, with every step.

Ava's family was huddled together, wide-eyed and cowering in the corner. The girls, who were just as surprised, stood frozen, confused.

"It's ok everyone," Ava assured them. "This is my family." Ava made her way over to them.

"You keep your family in the basement?" Olga asked shocked.

"No, Olga." Ava smiled. "I snuck them in last night."

"But why?" Heidi asked. "How did you know there would be a raid?"

"I didn't. Not exactly -"

There was a loud explosion, the force of which rattled the house above them. Ava looked up, hoping the structure and all the supports would hold. At least long enough for the bombing to cease.

"Everyone, over here, now!" Ava motioned for the girls to join her and her family. They huddled together in the dim basement light as the bombing continued. Some close. Some far away. All of them hitting their target. A constant pummel on the city of Dresden that Ava couldn't help but feel partially responsible for.

13th February, 11:53pm

Ava's head snapped up for the third time as she fought to stay awake. Joseph and Levi slept huddled around Ayala who refused to rest no matter how much Ava insisted. Hila was leaning her head against the back wall, eyes closed, although Ava was sure her mother was far from sleeping. No doubt she was deep in prayer.

Heidi, Olga and Tilly all slept restlessly, every bump or creek causing a stir. Margot sat silently beside Ava, wide awake but lost in thought. Ayala released a yawn, drawing Ava's attention.

"Ayala," Ava whispered. "Rest, please. I promise to wake you if anything happens." Ava insisted again, although she knew she wouldn't need to, the bombing would do that all on its own. Ayala looked at her, her gaze saying more than her mouth. "Maybe for a little while." She reluctantly agreed and rested her head against the wall behind her, shifting Levi slightly in her lap.

The basement was plunged into a silence that was heavy with uncertainty. Ava's mind drifted back again to the altercation in the alleyway between her and Richter. If he came back, it would mean the end of her. There was no going back to life before this night, regardless of who won the war. There was no way Richter would let her live when the air raid was done. She was going to have to get her family out of Dresden regardless of the risk of exposure. Unless.

Unless Nathan and Eddie kept their word. All of her hope rested on two men she barely knew and a God she wasn't sure she believed in.

The sound of a door closing broke through Ava's thoughts and woke everyone from their restless sleep. Ava and Margot exchanged worried glances as Ava stood, putting a finger to her lips, telling them all to be silent. She grabbed a hammer from the toolbox and made her way up the stairs towards the door, pressing her ear to it, listening. The footsteps were heavy causing Ava's stomach to drop in fear at the thought it could be Richter coming back to finish what he started. The footsteps moved carefully through the kitchen and into the saloon. The floorboards creaked as the intruder made their way up the stairs. Ava's heart pounded in her ears, but she remained still, breathing as quietly and as steady as she could. A few moments later, the footsteps returned to the kitchen, gradually getting louder as they approached the pantry where the basement door was hidden.

Ava readied the hammer in her hand.

"Olga?" A raspy voice whispered low. "Olga, are you in there?"

"Otto?" Ava whispered back, confused and equally delighted.

"Ja! Ava?" Otto asked, as she opened the door to see the garbage man, covered in soot and dust but sporting his typical grin.

"Quick, quick, come in. Olga is in here with us." Ava ushered Otto in, locking the door behind them. Olga was immediately in Otto's arm, the two hugging in relief that the other was safe.

"Ohh, Otto, mein Liebchen! I thought you were lost!" Olga exclaimed, showering the man with kisses.

"I almost was! But luckily I was on the outskirts of town when the bombing started and I was able to find shelter in a barn. But there was no way I was leaving my little schnappsie!" He planted a kiss on her lips and suddenly realised he had an audience.

"Entschuldigen sie!" Otto stepped back from Olga, pink filling his cheeks.

"It's fine Otto, this is my mother, sister and two nephews." Ava smiled at the man's embarrassment.

"Guten Abend." Otto tipped his head towards Ava's family.

"Otto, what is it like outside?" Olga asked.

"Bad, very bad. Many wounded, too many for the hospital. Most of the north side of the city seems to be destroyed. All the factories. People are looting. It is chaos. Which is why I came for you, mein Liebchen, we should leave. Now." Otto grabbed Olga's hand.

"No, wait!" Ava stepped in front of them. "It's not safe. They will bomb again."

"What makes you say that?" Olga asked, eyes wide with growing fear.

"Because -" Ava stopped herself, unsure if the girls would understand if she revealed how she knew...and why she had not told them sooner. "Because that's what they do. They'll lull you into a false sense of security so you think it's safe to leave and then they bomb again." Ava looked between Otto and Olga, hoping they would believe her.

"Oh Otto, maybe we should not go?" Olga looked, pleadingly.

"Schnappsie if we wait we may get bombed anyway! Plus there is not enough room down here for us all. I have a brother just across the border. I heard that they have pulled the Nazi soldiers patrolling the borders from their posts as reinforcements. We have a window of time to make it across without papers. We can cross through the forest and be there in a day or two. But we need to leave now." He pleaded. Olga paused for a moment, the wheels turning in her head.

"Ok, Otto, I will come with you." Olga nodded eagerly and picked up her coat.

"Take me with you?" Tilly stood up, desperation lacing her voice. "I don't want to risk being bombed or buried alive."

"Me too?" Heidi asked, quickly standing next to Tilly, fear evident in their eyes. Olga looked pleadingly at Otto.

"Ja, ja. Ok. Quick." Otto replied.

"Ava, I'm sorry…there's barely enough room for us all. Now might be our only chance." Tilly looked apologetically at her.

Ava paused, wanting to fight, wanting to convince them to stay but she could see their fear. Maybe it was better if they got out of Dresden. She sighed. "It's fine, Tilly. I understand." She held her arms out and hugged the shaking girl. "You be safe, ok? You too Heidi." She looked over at Otto. "Take care of my girls." Otto nodded, helping Olga with her coat and tipping his hat in the direction of Ava's family. They made their way upstairs, Ava kissed each of them on the cheek as they scurried out of the basement and into the night. Locking the door behind them, Ava prayed for their safety, something she seemed to be doing more and more these days.

She made her way back down the stairs, her heart breaking when she saw the fear in the eyes of her family, causing her to question whether or not they should have gone with Otto too. But Nathan had told her to remain inside. All she could do was hope he was a man of his word and trust that Yahweh, despite all her doubt, loved her family enough to protect them.

A loud explosion rattled the building above them. Ava rushed to her family.

"That sounded like it was right above us." Margot whispered. She looked at Ava as they huddled together, both thinking the same fearful thought.

"They're as good as gone." Ayala commented, just as another bomb dropped. They all screamed this time, dust falling on them from the floorboards above.

"All we can do is pray they somehow made it out in time." Ava replied, looking out the small basement window, her words portraying a hope she did not possess. The sound of footsteps in the alleyway and a woman screaming grew louder. Ava caught their shadows as they passed the basement. She covered Levi's ears, trying to shield him from the pain and fear of the screaming.

Another bomb dropped close by, causing the house to shake like it never had before. More dust and debris fell from the floor above them, tins of food and supplies rolled off the shelf across from the huddled group. Ava grabbed a blanket and spread it out over them, the group huddling beneath it. The pounding of the bombs continued, the explosions mixed with the sound of a city on fire.

Ava tried to calm her heart which was pounding in her ears, when she realised the air was filled with the whisperings of another sound. She strained to locate the origin and realised it was coming from within the basement. She lifted her head, meeting her mother's gaze. Hila was singing. She lifted her eyes towards the heavens and closed them as she opened her mouth and allowed the song she would sing to her daughters whenever they were scared, fill the basement.

God is our refuge and strength,

An ever-present help in trouble.

Therefore we will not fear

Though the earth give way

And the mountains fall into the sea

Though waters roar and foam

And the mountains quake in their surging

We will not fear

We will not fear

The Lord Almighty is with us

He is our fortress

He is our rock

He is our God.

The familiarity of the song quietened Ava's heart. Her mother's ability to press into Yahweh in such deep times of need always amazed her. Such faith was hard to ignore. Drawn in by the melody, Ava found herself quietly singing along with her mother. Ayala soon joined as they huddled together amidst the uncertainty and fear, clinging to each other. The bombing and screaming continued but their awareness of it faded into the background. Memories from a time Ava had buried deep inside her began to play. A time when she had believed in the God she was singing about right now. A time when it all had seemed simple and safe. And though she would never confess to it, a flicker of faith in a God Ava had long forgot, began to glow deep inside her and she rested in its warmth.

FOURTEEN

The Need for Coffee

1 **4th February 2:03am**

All was silent again. The singing had ceased. Sleep had finally found its way into their weary souls. Only Ava remained awake, unable to settle her mind long enough to find the peace sleep offered. Rolling waves of fear, worry and guilt unceasingly washed over her. Fear over Richter coming back and finding her and her family. Worry over their safety and whether or not they should have left with Otto. Guilt over not having told those she claimed to care for about the bombing.

"You should try to rest, Hadar." Hila whispered.

"I thought you were asleep." Ava whispered back.

"Oh my girl, old age took a solid night's sleep away from me many years ago. I wake up many times through out the night."

"How do you find any rest?" Ava rested her head against the wall and closed her eyes briefly, thankful for the reprieve the conversation offered from the rolling swell of emotions she was treading water in.

"I pray. Always pray." Hila smiled.

"What do you pray about?" Ava asked, more to keep the conversation going then out of any real curiosity.

"Everything. I pray for our boys, that Yahweh will keep them safe and help them to grow up big and strong. I pray for Benjamin, that one day he will return to us. I pray for Ayala and the hardness in her heart. I pray for your father, asking God to pass on messages for me." Ava could hear the smile in Hila's tone. Her mother's never-ending love for her father warmed Ava's heart. "Mostly I pray for you." Ava looked at her mother.

"Me?"

Hila nodded.

"Oh Mama, you don't need to worry about me." Ava brushed Hila's comment aside, the care in it making her feel oddly uncomfortable.

"How can I not?" Hila asked. "You have burdened yourself with the job of protecting this family. A burden that should not have been yours to carry." Hila sighed. "I failed you after your father died. I failed us all. And by doing so, sent you to a life of this." Hila motioned with her eyes to the building above them. "I blame myself for you ending up here."

Ava's heart twisted in her chest. "Mama, please don't blame yourself. My decisions are my own."

"But the motivation for those decisions was caused by me." Hila stared out the small basement window as the ghosts of past pain crept in through the silence that now sat between them. Ava's heart broke over her mother's unfounded guilt. Especially when it wasn't Hila's fault at all.

"We cannot change the past." Hila finally broke the silence. "And while I will always find it hard to accept what you do, tonight, I am grateful for the way it just may have saved us all."

Ava looked at her mother, unable to hide her surprise at her comment. Hila's face softened, a small smile forming across her lips. "Ava, my darling, if you had not owned this brothel you would not have met Richter, or the spies. You wouldn't have known about the bombing and you wouldn't have been able to bring us to safety." Hila sighed. "Sometimes, what seems like a bad thing, God can turn into good." She paused. "And I think he has done that here."

Ava felt a tear slide down her cheek and instinctively reached for her mother's hand. While there was so much yet to say, so many years of hurt and pain that needed to be healed, Ava instead said what was needed.

"I love you, Mama."

"I love you too, my daughter."

14th February, 3:24pm.

To: Agent Sinclair

From: Secretary of State for Air, Sir Sinclair.

Subject: Re - Operation Thunderclap

Final bombing of Dresden scheduled for midday 15th February. Urgently return to London for next assignment. You should have been on the train from Paris yesterday.

. . .

Nathan released a frustrated sigh.

"What's the verdict then?" Eddie asked as he lit a cigarette.

"Final bombing will be tomorrow. Midday." Nathan replied.

"Really?" Eddie's eyes grew wide in surprise. "Wouldn't think there was much left to bomb after the roasting they've already given it."

"Yeah, roasting is right given the number of incendiaries they've dropped. They want to make sure the munitions factory is well and truly buried...along with the entire population of Dresden, it would seem." Nathan's annoyance grew stronger. "For all our talk of being on the side of right, you would think that we would know when to stop...some days I wonder if we're just as bad as them." He looked out over the Lusatian Neisse River.

Nathan had managed to keep them in Görlitz for a few extra days, convincing Eddie they needed a break. It wasn't hard, the Irishman loved his booze and women, and both could be found in Görlitz. But now that he knew when the final bombing was going to be, he had no reason to wait any longer.

"Right. Well it's time to get going. Come on Flannagen." Nathan said, heading down the street.

"Back to London we go."

"We're not going to London." Nathan replied, his mind set on the destination.

"Where are we going then?" A confused Eddie fell in step beside him.

"Dresden."

"What!?" Eddie grabbed Nathan's arm. "No, old chap. I'm not walking into a death trap. Every Nazis in that city could still be looking for us. We're dead men walking if we cross back over now."

Eddie folded his arms in defiance. "You're right daft, you know that?"

"I have to go back. I promised." Nathan looked at Eddie. "Look, I know it's a risk. I know we could be heading to our deaths and if you choose not to come, there will be no hard feelings. But I can't leave her there. Not when she risked so much to save us. If it wasn't for her, we wouldn't have made it out of Dresden alive."

"But you pledged your allegiance to the British flag first. Your loyalties don't lie with a German Jew." Eddie shot back.

"What I pledged allegiance to is the protection of all mankind. Not just the ones we choose to protect. I'm going back." Fuelled by determination, Nathan continued towards the flat.

"You won't make it back before the bombing." Eddie yelled after him.

"I'm not trying to. I promised I'd come for her and her family after the final bombing, I now know when that will be." Nathan called over his shoulder. "God, please let them still be alive." He whispered to the sky, setting his mind to the mission ahead.

He heard footsteps coming up behind him, a panting Eddie appearing in his peripherals. Nathan glanced at Eddie.

"I can't let you go alone, now can I?" He caught his breath. "Besides, we both know your German sucks."

15th February, 11:43am

Ava slowly stirred as the smell of coffee and damp filled her nostrils. Flashes of bombs and screams came crashing in triggering a rush of adrenalin to flood her veins, waking her fully. She sat up, trying to take in her surroundings.

Her nephews were playing in the corner. Ayala was reading an old newspaper while Hila knitted. Any other day, this would have seemed normal. But Margot.

"Margot? Where's Margot?" Ava rasped, her throat dry from the dust and lack of sleep.

"She is just making coffee upstairs." Ayala replied, lowering the paper.

"Upstairs? No, we're not supposed to leave!" Panic rippled through Ava's body.

"It's ok, she's just up the stairs." Ayala tried to soothe. "If anyone comes or if there is any more bombings, she will come straight back down."

Ava went to stand, suddenly becoming aware of the blanket that was covering her and her mother's coat that was bundled up where her head had been resting. "I must have fallen asleep." She mumbled to herself, annoyed she had been so weak. She needed to be strong. She needed to keep them all safe. They were relying on her.

"You needed the rest, Ava." Ayala shifted her weight, sitting beside her sister. "It's been over 24 hours since the last bombing. Hopefully that means it has stopped."

"That's one day down…" Ava trailed off. "Only two more to go."

"Are you sure he said three days?" Ayala asked. "It has been over 24 hours, chances are they won't bomb again."

"He said 3 days, Ayala." Ava glanced up at the small basement window. "We need to wait three days from the last bombing and then he'll come for us."

"What if he doesn't come?"

Ava sighed. The thought had crossed her mind more than once but something within her kept them locked in this basement. She wouldn't rest properly until the third day.

"We'll do as your sister says, Ayala. She's kept us safe thus far, we have no reason to question her now. Or her British friend." Hila chimed in, not taking her eyes off her knitting. Ava smiled at her mother who, even now, still had the ability to silence a disagreement between Ava and her sister.

"Ava?" Ayala shuffled closer to her sister.

"Yes?" Ava replied, closing her eyes, not trying to hide the weariness she felt over having to defend herself yet again to Ayala's disappointment in her life.

"Margot told me everything. And I just wanted to say…that… well…I'm sorry." Ava's eyes shot open. "What exactly did she tell you?"

"About the spies and that day with Joseph. How you hid them. How that man has been blackmailing you…what you've had to go through…how you've kept us safe." Ayala kept her eyes low. "I said some horrible things…"

"It's fine, little sister." Ava tilted Ayala's chin towards her, meeting her eyes. "We are all still here and that's what matters." A forgiving smile formed on Ava's lips that mirrored Ayala's. Ava wrapped an arm around her sister and gave her shoulder a squeeze. Her gaze found the bottom of the staircase, drawing her thoughts up the steps to the basement door.

"I should check on Margot." Ava released her arm from her sister's shoulder and stood, stretching her tired body, the nights of sleeping on the ground taking their toll. Ava longed for a hot bath and her warm, comfortable bed. If it was still there. She wearily made her way up the stairs, carefully opening the door. Debris from the broken windows and shattered plates and cups littered the kitchen. Somehow, despite the obvious destruction, the building was still standing. A miracle in itself.

Ava scanned the room, realising the kitchen was empty.

"Margot?" Ava started to pick her way around the debris, noticing the back door was open. The kettle sat silent on the stove. Why on earth did Margot think there would still be gas connected at the house?

"Margot! Margot!" Ava called out, panic beginning to rise as her eyes fell on a piece of paper on the table.

Gone to get firewood to start the stove. Didn't want to wake you.

Be back soon.

M x

Ava's heart dropped. The old stove could still be lit manually but they hadn't done so in years.

Ava went to the back door, her breath catching in her chest as she surveyed for the first time the destruction that surrounded her. Entire streets of houses, gone. Flattened. Steal and rubble littered with clothes, pots, a broken bed frame and a stuffed animal were the only indicators that anything other than destruction had ever existed there. Smoke billowed out across the skyline and smouldering embers flickered and burned, signalling the carnage. And death. Ava suddenly could see the bodies amongst the rubble. The smell of burning flesh hung in the air. She choked on the soot and stench, overwhelmed by what her city had been reduced to. Tears slid down her dirt stained cheeks, an overwhelming sense of guilt surged from within. She should have told more people about the raids, she should have warned the town. Why hadn't she tried to save more people? What of every other mother, father, daughter or son in Dresden? Did they not deserve to live?

A familiar sound in the distance caught Ava's attention, amplifying the fear already consuming her body.

"No…" She whispered, panic rising as what was left of the air raid sirens wailed out across the mass grave of Dresden.

"Margot!! MARGOT!!!" Ava screamed, launching herself forward in pursuit of her friend. But something grabbed her arm, pulling her back inside. Ava turned to see her mother fiercely holding onto her.

"No Mama!! I have to find Margot! Let me go!" Ava turned back to the door. "MARGOT!" She screamed.

"No my girl, come back!" Hila gripped Ava tighter. "Margot will find shelter but you will be of no use to anyone if you are blown to pieces."

The sound of the bombs dropping ricocheted across the sky.

"No, Mama!! I have to find her!!" Ava pulled her arm from her mother's grip and ran back to the door. "MARGO-"

FIFTEEN

The Return

1 **6th February, 8:34am**

Ava's eyes flung open, her mind surging into a frenzy, trying to piece together why her head throbbed and her body wouldn't move. Margot!....Where was Margot!? She coughed, sending stinging currents of pain through her lungs as she tried to sit up.

"Mar.." She tried to speak but her voice failed her, the sound lodged in her sandpaper throat..

"Shhh, sh, shh. It's ok. Just lie back down." Ayala placed her hands on Ava's shoulders, gently guiding her back to the makeshift bed.

"Wha...what...happened?" She managed to whisper. Ayala picked up a cup of water, lifting it to Ava's lips. She drank deeply, the cool liquid triggering a mingled sensation of relief and pain in her raw throat.

"There. That's it. Drink a little more." Ayala kept the cup to Ava's lips as she quenched her thirst. "Your body is going to need some time, so don't try and get up. You took quite a hit when that bomb landed in the alley."

"Mama!" Panic rose in Ava's stomach as flashes of her mother trying to pull her back inside flooded her memory.

"I am fine, mein Liebchen." Hila crouched down beside her. Ava could see little cuts flanking the right side of her mother's face, the bruising of a black eye colouring her face. "You took the brunt of the explosion."

"What happened?" Ava managed to choke out.

"You ran back to the door to find Margot when a bomb went off not far from the house. The force of the explosion sent us both flying backwards. You hit your head on the table and have quite a few cuts and bruises from the shattered glass and debris."

"And Margot?" Ava didn't miss the worried glance shared between her sister and mother. "She has still not returned." Hila lovingly stroked the top of Ava's head. Ava bit her lip, trying to keep the tears at bay but she couldn't hold it back any longer. Grief overwhelmed her and she let the tears come, sobbing into her mother's embrace.

"It's all my fault, Mama, it's all my fault…"

"No, Hadar, you couldn't have stopped Margot."

"I shouldn't have fallen asleep…I shouldn't have made us stay…it's all my fault." Tears flooded Ava's eyes, visions of a burning Dresden flickering through her mind. "I've sentenced us all to death…I should have …"

"Ava," Ayala tilted Ava's face towards her own, locking eyes. "There are things you can control and there are things you can not. And I would know. If I could have prevented Benjamin from leaving that morning to go find work, I would have. But he was determined to go." Ayala took a breath, pushing her own tears of grief away. "There's no way you could've prevented the bombing. But what you could do, what you did do, was keep your family alive and safe. Margot's decision to leave the house is not your fault. You can't control everything."

Ayala's words did little to settle the turmoil in Ava's heart. Hila gripped her daughter tighter. "It's ok Hadar, it's going to be ok."

In that moment, repulsion at her real name surged from within Ava. How many more people had to die on her watch? It seemed she was destined to repeat her mistakes, regardless of how far she ran from the little girl beside the barn.

"It's Ava, Mama. My name is Ava." She corrected, detaching herself again from a name that spoke of death.

"No, my girl. You are my daughter and I gave you the name Hadar. You will always be my Hadar." Hila gently rocked Ava back and forth.

"You wouldn't want her as your daughter if you knew what she had done." The words had slipped out of Ava's mouth before she even realised what she was saying.

"Oh my girl, I don't like how you have lived your life but that doesn't mean I will ever stop wanting you as my daughter." Hila tried to soothe Ava's pain.

"That's not what I meant…" Ava sniffed, removing herself from her mother's embrace, unable to be close to the heart she had caused so much pain.

"What do you mean then?"

Ava sighed, her eyes instinctively drawn to the window of the basement. Shimmers of a little red bird in the alleyway flittered through her mind causing an unusual peace to settle in her heart. She could taste the truth lingering at the tip of her tongue and rather than swallow it, as she had many times before, she decided to release it. The chances of her family making it out alive were diminishing as quick as the wax on the candles they had lit, so why not confess and end this life with a little peace.

"I'm the reason Papa is dead. I killed him." She let the truth spill from her lips, allowing it to flood the room with all the guilt and regret she had dammed up inside her heart all these years.

"What?" Hila whispered, shock and confusion choking the volume from her voice. "What do you mean? The barn collapsed on its own, how could you have caused that?"

"It was my fault he was in the barn in the first place." Ava took a deep breath and released the dam of truth. "That day, I was laying in the field behind the old barn, watching the clouds. It was getting late and I knew I needed to come home but it was such a beautiful, warm summer afternoon. I didn't want to leave. Papa came looking for me. I thought he would be so angry when he found me, but instead he laid down in the grass beside me, watching the clouds roll by, pointing out different animals that the clouds were making." Ava's heart broke all over again as the memory played like a movie, projecting from the deep recesses of her mind. "Then a Rosenfink landed not far from us. I wanted one so badly so I tried to catch it. It flew off into the old barn and I went after it. Papa told me to not go in but I didn't listen. I followed the bird in and found it perched on the loft." She took a breath, stabilising the tears that were beginning to stain her cheeks. "I started to climb the ladder when Papa pulled me off. He said it wasn't safe up there and that we needed to get home. I looked up in the direction of the bird and then back at him. He sighed, kissed my head and said he would try. So he climbed the ladder, edging closer and closer to the bird, when there was this big cracking sound. He yelled at me to get out. I said not without him. Then there was another crack." Ava's voice broke. "He looked me in the eye and said 'Mein Liebchen, I will be right behind you'. So I turned and ran. And just as I made it out the door, there was a third loud crack and the loft gave way, bringing the rest of the barn with it ." Ava paused, keeping her eyes locked on the ground, she couldn't handle the anger that would greet them if she raised her gaze. "It's my fault he is dead. I'm the reason he was in the barn."

Hila reached for her daughter but Ava shifted away, repelled by any sort of kindness her mother might be offering. "Don't Mama. I don't deserve your compassion."

"Hadar…"

"No. Don't say her name." Ava flared. "That's the name of the girl who killed her father. But Ava…Ava…Ava has…" She gave over to the tears burning the backs of her eyes. "I'm so sorry Mama, I'm so, so sorry." She sobbed, allowing the shame to purge. Ava felt her mother's arms wrap around, holding her tight. The long-held guilt poured forth, coupled with the fear of Margot being lost and the pain of causing her family so much grief. It was all too much.

Hila's embrace softened as she gently moved Ava out of her arms, tilting Ava's chin so that their eyes met.

"My daughter, I want you to listen to me and listen well." Hila caught her daughter's attention with the firm yet compassionate tone of her voice. "Your father loved his family more than anything. He would have done anything for you, for us. That day, in the barn, is just another example of the lengths he would go to make his daughter happy. It was foolish of him to climb a ladder in a loft he knew was unstable. But your father was just as stubborn as you are and would not have listened if any of us had tried to stop him." Hila's face softened, tears quietly slipping down her cheeks. "This is not your fault. It's not even your father's fault. It was simply a very sad and tragic accident. So, my daughter, you need to forgive yourself because none of us blame you or hold you accountable for what happened that day. Not even God."

Ava wiped the tears from her eyes. She had held responsibility for the death of her father for so long, she didn't know how to receive the forgiveness her mother was offering her. But in the smallest recesses of her soul, she felt something new begin to replace the guilt and shame, something that felt a little like grace. Hila pulled her daughter into her embrace again.

"Whatever name you choose," She whispered to Ava's hair. "Know that neither of them represent a woman who is guilty." Hila tucked a strand of hair behind her ear. Ava felt the grip around her body intensify as her sister and her nephews encircled her. For the first time, in a long time, Ava allowed herself to be loved.

16th February, 10:13am

From: Frankland.

To: Secretary of State for Air, Sir Sinclair.

Subject: Operation Thunderclap.

Success! The German city of Dresden is flattened, the secret munitions factory has been annihilated and the German war effort further crippled. God is shining upon us!

Nathan and Eddie stood in silence. Their eyes frantically scanned the ruins of a once thriving city. Rubble, dust and dirt were mingled with blood, tears and decaying flesh. Death was not hidden neatly in the ground, instead it laid bare for all to see. Dresden was an inside out graveyard.

Those still breathing sifted through the remains like vultures, scurrying into the shadows when they caught sight of Nathan and Eddie as they began to pick their way over the blown apart bricks and mortar. Smoked billowed into the sky, marking smouldering messes of shops, offices and homes. Something cracked beneath Nathan's foot. He glanced down, a picture frame still holding the image of a smiling family stared back at him. The surge of guilt he had been fighting since they could see Dresden on the horizon flooded his gut again. How much of this was he responsible for? Pushing the thought aside, he continued to carefully climb over the remains of Dresden.

Most of the landmarks and streets they would have used to find their way to the Zwinger were gone. Instinct would have to be their guide. Staying South of the Elbe and the fields to their left, they moved as fast as they could, stopping to see if there were survivors in the hollowed buildings that remained. Few were found, understandably suspicious of two men who externally appeared unaffected by the bombing. Their help was not wanted.

"Maybe we'd be better off focussing on the ones we came to find." Nathan mumbled to himself, watching fearful eyes scuttle away into the smoke.

"There it is." Eddie commented, pointing off in the distance. Nathan looked up. "Yeah, I think you're right." He replied picking up his pace, a glimmer of hope beginning to build.

As they drew closer, Nathan could begin to make out the features of the Zwinger. Most of the windows shattered, pieces of shrapnel were lodged in its facade, the balcony had fallen down completely. And yet, the building itself remained standing.

"Have you ever seen....?" Eddie asked, stopping a few meters short of the remains.

"No, never." Nathan stopped beside him. "I honestly thought that coordinates alone would not have saved this place...it's like there was something protecting it..."

"Somehow, by the grace of God, it's still standing." Eddie mumbled.

"By the grace of God is right, old chap." Nathan studied the building. "But you know what that means?" Nathan smiled at Eddie. "There's a really good chance she's still alive."

Nathan hurriedly scrambled his way over the rubble, making his way to the back door.

"The door! It's open!" He called back to Eddie, hoping that it didn't mean Ava had left already...or worse.

"Woah, careful there, mate. You don't want to be the reason that building comes down." Eddie called out as he followed Nathan over the unstable ground.

Nathan arrived at the doorway and paused, taking in the sight. From where he was standing, he could see the roof had partially collapsed in the main saloon. Shards of plates, cups, bowls and debris covered the floor. A broken beam blocked access to the basement doorway, sealing the entryway. Nathan stepped into the room as Eddie placed a hand on his shoulder, stopping him from going any further. "Just go steady mate. It's still standing, but not for long." Eddie motioned towards the cracked main support beam holding up the second floor. "If that breaks, this whole building will come down on us."

Nathan nodded as the two men cautiously made their way towards the basement.

"On my count." Nathan said, as they each took a side of the heavy beam. "One...two...three." They heaved the beam up, causing the house to creak and shift. They held they breath and looked around, waiting to see if the house would settle or bury them.

"We don't have much time." Eddie whispered. Nathan nodded and the two put their weight behind the bean, pushing it up and away from the door, laying it on the ground as quickly and gently as possible.

"Who's there?" a muffled voice on the other side of the door demanded.

Nathan's heart exploded in his chest. "Ava?"

"Nathan?"

"Yes, Ava. Open the door." He urged, eager to see her.

Silence. "How do I know it's you?" A wary voice met his request.

"Because I have this." Nathan reached into his shirt pocket, his fingers finding the Rosenfink brooch he had kept safely close to his heart since she had dropped it into his hand the night they had escaped. He knelt down and slid the pin under the door. "Rosenfink." He whispered, placing a hand on the door. He waited in the silence. A few inches separated them, his only hope of bridging the distance was a little brooch with a bird on it. Would it be enough after all they had been through?

The click clack of a lock being released freed a breath from Nathan's chest he hadn't realised he was holding. The door slowly creaked open revealing a scratched and bruised Ava. Her cheeks had tear tracks forged through the dirt on her face. She was not the pristine Golden Goddess he had met that first night but the strength that her face now showed took Nathan's breath away. To him, she had never looked more beautiful.

"Is it safe?" She asked, her eyes darting around the room.

"Yes, but we need to move now." Nathan reached out his hand, desperate to take her safety. "The whole house could collapse any moment."

Ava didn't take his hand, instead turning towards the basement. "It's ok. It's him." She turned back to face him. He wasn't quite sure what about her was different but it was more than the dirt and dust she was covered in. Something about her seemed lighter.

"I was beginning to wonder if you would come." She confessed, drawing his focus.

"I was always coming back for you." Nathan replied, his words causing a faint smile o form at the corners of Ava's mouth. He smiled back.

Out of the darkness of the basement emerged Levi, Joseph, Ayala and Hila, clearly eager to be released.

"Margot?" Eddie asked, looking past Ava's family. Ava looked into his eyes and gently shook her head. "I don't know…" Was all she could muster as a big crack rang out and the house shifted violently.

"We gotta go. Now!" Eddie picked up Levi and led the way. Joseph followed closely as Ava turned to help Hila up the final stair. "Come Mama." She urged trying to quicken her pace.

"I've got her." Nathan stepped around her and picked Hila up in his arms. The house began to rattle and groan.

"GO!" Ava commanded.

"Not without you!" Nathan protested.

"AVA!" Hila panicked.

"I'm right behind you! RUN!" Ava yelled as the beam above them finally succumbed to weight baring down on it, dust and debris filling the room. Nathan made it out the door just as the house caved in, the crash echoing across the empty skyline. He gently put Hila down, frantically turning back, his eyes scanning for any sign of Ava.

"Ava! Ava!" He called out, tripping and scrambling back towards the house, Eddie and Ayala followed close behind. The cloud of dust created by the collapse lazily settled revealing a decimated, mangled remnants of a building. Panic flooded Nathan's body. He began to pull at splintered wood and broken beams, joined by Eddie and Ayala, calling for Ava.

"Where is she!?" Ayala screamed.

"I don't know - she was right behind me!" Nathan yelled back. "Ava! AVA!"

"Shut it!" Eddie demanded, stopping his digging. Nathan and Ayala paused, confused by his demand. "Listen." In the eery silence they held their breath and listened. Tension clung to the settling dust, but all was silent. Muscles twitched at the ready, anticipating hurried movement, but all was quiet. Ears strained to hear the faintest cry for help over the pounding of their anxious hearts, but no such cry was there to be heard.

The trio cast worried glances as the seconds ticked over into minutes.

Ayala's eyes grew wide. "There, over there! I heard a cough!" She yelled, scrambling over the debris, Nathan and Eddie close behind. Ayala stopped at what was left of the back door. "It was somewhere here." She whispered, all three pausing again in the hopes of hearing signs of life beneath the ruins.

The peaceful suspended darkness only lasted a few minutes, a sense of weightlessness surrounding her. She wanted to stay. It felt safe. It felt free. It felt like home. But consciousness grabbed hold of Ava and at a head-spinning speed, dragged her back to reality.

Her eyes flung open, her lungs aggressively sucking in a breath, filling the void in her chest and sending shooting pain everywhere. She coughed and moaned, still trying to gain her bearings.

"She's under the door!" She heard a muted male voice yell and wondered who was under a door and why? Suddenly light pierced the darkness with such force it made Ava nauseous. She defensively lifted her arms to shield her from whatever was coming. Instead, she felt hands gently slid under her shoulders.

"Ava." The tone of voice became familiar, triggering memories from the last few weeks to play in her mind at rapid speed like a movie on fast forward. She felt the strong arms beneath her lift her body, sending sharp, dizzying pain through her right ankle.

"My ankle!" Ava rasped. "My ankle is stuck."

"The beam, it's pinning her ankle." Eddie placed a hand either side of the beam and pulled, the old wooden log barely moving an inch.

"Ayala, hold Ava under her shoulders and pull when we tell you to." Ava felt the strong arms leave, replaced by the familiarity of her sister's embrace.

"I got you." The comfort those three words from Ayala brought to Ava's heart caused tears to prick at the back of her eyes.

"On my count." Nathan instructed, readying himself at the other end of the beam. "One, two, three." The two men heaved the beam up as Ayala pulled Ava out from underneath it. Dropping the beam, Nathan raced back to Ava, scooping her up in his arms and carrying her to the safety of the street. He gently placed her down beside Hila.

"Oh mein Liebchen." Hila whispered, stroking Ava's face. "I thought I had lost you."

"You could never lose me, Mama." Ava coughed, wincing at the pain that nudged at her side. Nathan kneeled beside her, sliding his hand around her neck and tipping a canteen of water to her lips. Ava welcomed the soothing sensation the liquid as it slid down her throat. Nathan let her take a few sips before wetting the sleeve of his shirt, wiping the dust covering her face. She hadn't felt kindness like this from a man since her father, the thought causing a lump to form in her throat. Her eyes met with his as he rubbed the cloth over her cheek.

"Thank you." She whispered. "For coming back."

"I was always coming back for you." He smiled, pushing a stray strand of hair from her face. "Nothing could have stopped me." Ava looked deep into his eyes, searching for a hint of falsehood but found only genuineness to his words. He meant it, he really meant it. They lingered in each other's eyes for a moment, exchanging whispers of desires too infant to give voice to.

"Do you think you can stand up?" Nathan asked, both of them becoming aware that they were sharing this moment with others.

"I think so." Ava pushed herself up, leaning into Nathan as he lift her to her feet. She winced, pain shooting through her ankle under her weight. "We're going to need to splint and wrap that." Eddie commented, picking up a piece of wood and opening his pack to find the first aid kit. Nathan lowered Ava onto a set of stairs that a few days ago had led to a house. Ava looked up, only a corner remained of what would have been a lovely home and probably a lovely family.

The sensation of Eddie splinting her ankle brought Ava's focus back. "It will do for now but we'll need to get you to a field hospital as soon as we can." Eddie tied off the bandage and stood.

Silence drifted into the ragged group, all of them unsure what to do or say as the gravity of what could have been settled amongst them. Ava's eyes were instinctively drawn to where the Zwinger once stood. It now joined the rest of the city as a pile of rubble and brokenness. It reminded her of the barn.

"Any longer down there and we would have all perished when the building collapsed." Hila whispered to the dust.

"Just like Papa, in the barn." Ayala muttered, unaware of how the words landed like a punch in Ava's chest. "Only this time, we're all alive." Ayala turned to face Ava. "And we have you to thank for that, Ava." She knew her sister was genuine in her thanks, but it did little to settle the troubled heart inside Ava.

"I'm so proud of you, mein Liebchen." Hila smiled at Ava. "You have fought so hard for us, to keep us safe and alive. And you did it."

"Almost…" Ava looked off towards the field. "I hope she is safe, wherever she is…" She whispered, wiping a tear that had escaped down her cheek.

"There wasn't supposed to be this much destruction." Nathan cut into the silence. "The 401st squadron missed the city centre because of the cloud coverage yesterday, bombing the south eastern suburbs instead." He looked at Ava. "I honestly thought the brothel would not be standing at all. I was surprised…and relieved." His expression softened. "Ava, I'm sorry, I never thought-"

"Nathan, please don't apologise." Ava cut off the unnecessary apology. "You kept us safe. If you hadn't told me about the bombing or what to do, then none of us would be standing here right now. We owe you our lives." She looked up into his eyes, caught off guard at how they made her lightheaded. Everything within her wanted to reach for him, to be pulled into his arms. But she kept her arms at her side, letting the feeling subside. Ava awkwardly stood, wanting to not feel so helpless. "I just wish I could have saved them all…" Taking a step, Ava stumbled slightly and found herself caught by Nathan's arms. He pulled her into his embrace, sending Ava's head spinning.

"This is not your fault." He said, holding her gaze. "The Allied forces were always going to bomb the city. You are, in no way, responsible for that decision." Nathan looked deep into Ava's eyes. She knew he was right but regret tugged at her heart. "I knew it was coming and I only thought about myself, about my family. I could have told more people…I should have…"

"Ava, you can't spend your life trying to atone for your past. You will never live long enough."

The truth of his statement was a deep revelation to Ava's soul. He was right. She had spent her entire adult life taking care of her family as a way of atoning for her past, for her father's death. The weight of such a burden was getting too heavy to carry.

"It's the only way I know how to make things right." She looked out over flattened skyline of Dresden and wondered how long it would take to make things right with the city.

"What if there was another way?"

Ava shot Nathan a questioning look, disbelief that such a way existed.

"What if you accepted the forgiveness offered you, knowing you can never fully make things right."

Ava looked away again, unable to face the truth in Nathan's comment. She knew what, or rather whom, he was referring to. For so long she had fought Him, abandoning God the way she felt he had abandoned her. If he was so powerful then why could he not have prevented the barn from falling. Or the sale of their home. Or the chance encounter she had with Sabine. Or provided another path to walk. The complexity of her emotions and all that had unfolded over the years was too much to unravel. She was proud of all she had accomplished, even if it was in a line of work Yahweh did not approve of. And yet it had been her basement they had hidden in. Her brothel the spies had wandered into. Her connection with Richter that had led to them standing here, alive.

Ava knew deep in her soul that she could never have orchestrated such a plan, so maybe, just maybe, Yahweh was at work somehow. And if he was at work, then maybe he did care enough about her to keep her alive. And if he cared that much, then maybe he really did forgive her. And maybe she could forgive herself.

'Yahweh?' Ava silently prayed. 'Can you forgive me?' She hesitantly asked, unsure if the God she had once been so close with would want to draw close again.

A flittering of movement in her peripherals caught Ava's attention, her eyes drawn to the flash of red. A little Rosenfink landed not far from her, hopping around on the broken bricks and debris. Ava watched in stunned silence. This bird had been present with her throughout this entire ordeal but in this moment, Ava felt like she was seeing the bird for the first time. Instead of seeing it as representing the presence of her father, she saw the presence of her Father. Yahweh had been with her this whole time. And He forgave her.

"Forgive yourself, my Liebchen." Hila appeared beside Ava, sliding her arm around her waist. "No one else is holding you to account, except you."

Ava nodded, her voice choked by the swelling emotions. In that moment, a weight felt like it dropped from her shoulders, a lightness she had not felt since she was a child. She turned into her mother's embrace and let the forgiveness she had been depriving herself of take over. She lingered in it for a moment, letting forgiveness water her tired soul.

Ava grew aware of the rest of the group. It was going to take time to rebuild her relationship with Yahweh just like it was going to take time to rebuild her life. But right now, they needed to figure out their next step. Ava released herself from her mother's embrace.

"We need to find shelter." Nathan commented, scanning the surrounding area. "And then tomorrow, we'll start the journey to the border." Nathan reached for Ava's hand. "And then you'll come home with me."

Ave met his gaze, confusion in her eyes. "Come home with you? To England?"

"Yes. Come with me to England. Bring your whole family. There's nothing left for you here."

"Nathan, it's not as simple as that…"

"Yes it is."

"No. It's not, Nathan." Ava sighed, running her eyes over the levelled city skyline. "I need to help them."

"But the Nazis-"

"Are on the road to defeat, correct? The bombing served its purpose. But the people of Dresden didn't deserve to be caught in the crossfire."

"Ava, you aren't responsible for the destruction or their deaths."

"I know." She replied, her resolve building. "But I can help them rebuild." She paused, a smile forming at the edges of her lips as the sensation of freedom from the past washed through her once more. "I can rebuild now."

Nathan placed a hand on each shoulder, turning her to face him. Ava looked deep into his eyes. "Take my family." She whispered.

"What?"

"Take my family to England and I will follow later." Ava replied, more and more confident of what she needed to do next. Nathan scanned her eyes, she could see the longing within his and hoped he could see it reflected in her own.

"How long?" He choked. "How long do you need?"

"As long as it takes." She reached into her pocket and pulled out the Rosenfink pin. "But I will come. I promise." She smiled lightly, pinning the brooch to his lapel. "And I always keep my promises."

Nathan drew her close, the flurry of energy between them growing stronger. "When you do arrive, I'm never letting you go, Ava." He whispered, lowering his lips towards hers.

"Hadar." She smiled, looking up into his eyes. "Call me Hadar."

Glossary

Given the setting of this book, certain German words are used throughout. Here is a short Glossary of the terms and their meaning.

Kolibri: Hummingbird.

Rosenfink: Rose Finch.

Zwinger: The kill zone situated between to walls usually lining a castle or town. During time of peace, it was used as a garden. It seemed an appropriate name given Ava's place of work and home, The Zwinger Bordell, was both a place of play and of deceit.

Goldene Götten: Golden Goddess.

Richter: German name that means Judge.

Tanté: Aunty.

Mein Liebchen: My sweetheart or my love.

Mein Lamm: My lamb.

Luftwaffe: German Airforce.

Truppen: Troops.

Jetzt: Now.

Proost: Cheers.

Orpo: Police.

Entschuldigung: Excuse me.

Untermensch: a Nazis term for non-Aryan people meaning "sub-human" or not worthy of life.

About the Author

Neri Morris is an inquisitive author and accidental entrepreneur. Story-telling runs through her veins along with a lot of coffee and a love for the ocean. Neri began her writing career in 2020 but has been mastering the art of story since birth. Her first book *"Single Me: Learning to Love the Unwanted Path of Singleness"* is an insightful, funny and challenging look at singleness in the modern day Christian context.

FORTIFIED is Neri's first fiction novel, with plenty more in the works.

To find out more about Neri and her upcoming books, head to nerimorris.com or visit the social links below.

Also by Neri Morris

All books are available at nerimorris.com

Single Me: Learning to Love the Unwanted Path of Singleness